A

Miracle

Christmas

A Novella By

Willis Baker

Cover by f/32photo

This novella is a work of fiction, the names, characters, places, and incidents are either the product of the author's imagination or purely fictitious. Any resemblance to actual persons, living or dead, events or locales is entirely coincidental.

ISBN-13:
978-1492225096

ISBN-10:
1492225096

A Willowwind Book
Knoxville, TN 865-776-4970

This book is dedicated to motherhood

"I

have

no greater

joy than to hear

that my children walk

in truth"
3 John 1:4

Part

A Holy Night

December, 1996
Market Street
Claremont, Tennessee

Meredith McClain scurried down the snowy sidewalk when her attention was drawn through the wrought iron fence and into central park where a girl, approximately 10 to 12 years of age, sat on a park bench, alone. An unexpected chill gripped Meredith, not for the frigid weather, but for the child, especially unaccompanied. The courthouse clock struck the half hour, reminding her she had a brief stop to make before returning to the office.

She paused at a small shop. The beveled glass sign above the door read, Class in Glass. She stamped snow from her boots and entered under the ping of an ornamental bell. The shop was warm, and a bouquet of pine and cinnamon curled Christmas nostalgia into the air. An aging, fashionably-dressed female clerk arranged exotic and expensive glass figurines on a shelf.

"Merry Christmas, Miss," she greeted.

Meredith loosened her scarf, flitting remnants of snow flakes glistening in her mix of the winter-blonde 'bob' that touched her shoulders. "Merry Christmas to you," she replied, hugging herself for warmth as she commenced to peruse the shelves of prismatic presentations.

"It's toasty in here; you'll warm up in no time. Anything in particular I can show you?"

"I'm looking for a hostess gift."

Promoting the hope of a sale to her already bright smile, the clerk tilted her head slightly: "Glass is class, and always appropriate."

Meredith reviewed the shelves of offerings, her smile approving, until the view through a window behind the shelves interrupted. Her smile disappeared, her forehead wrinkled with question, and the unexpected chill of moments earlier not only returned, but pushed her mind back to ten years earlier when she had lost both her husband and their only son in a winter accident. The intensity on Meredith's face was sufficient to provoke the clerk to ask: "Is anything wrong? You Look a little pale."

The tone of Meredith's was gripped with concern. "That girl on the bench is only a child, and obviously alone."

"I'm afraid she's a boy, Miss. He's been there the better part of the day. He comes in to warm himself then faithfully returns to the bench. I asked if he was expecting someone and he said he's waiting for his mother. With those golden locks and angelic face, he certainly is pretty enough to be a girl."

Meredith seemed to go into a trance, and the clerk again noticed. "Excuse me, but are you sure you are all right?"

Meredith broke her trance.

"I'm sorry, but I'm fine, thank you. I can't believe a mother would leave her child alone in a park any time, let alone in this kind of weather. He could freeze."

Meredith reestablished her composure and continued to a cabinet, examining the display of fine glass merchandise. An intricate piece drew her attention. "This warm-colored piece makes me think of spring, and in this cold winter that's a good thing."

The clerk cautiously retrieved Meredith's selection from the cabinet. "I think you're right; it's beautifully crafted, by Orient and Flume, and a popular piece, from the Hawthorne pattern, literally iridized inside and out."

A volley of praise followed.

"It's magnificent."

"It's electrifying."

"I'm sure it also commands a hefty price."

"I don't recall that being the case, so let's just see." The clerk noted a number on the bottom of the piece, selected a volume from several leather bound books on the shelves behind her, laid it on the counter in front of them, opened it, and flipped a few pages. "Yes. Here it is." She curled approval on her face. "This will be a pleasant surprise for you. It's very reasonably priced at $510."

Meredith swallowed. "Maybe, but that's still outside my budget."

"I certainly understand that," she said, momentarily placing her finger to her lips in thought, then retrieved another piece. "This is considerably less expensive but just as comforting and beautiful, a Steinbach piece, crystal, named, *Lighthouse,* an excellent buy at $85."

Meredith caressed the rectangular piece, a lighthouse embedded in clear, solid crystal. Meredith was instantly in deep thought. "The Lighthouse" is my favorite inspirational song," she said quietly.

Meredith handed the clerk her credit card, her attention again drawn through the window into the park and to the boy child hunkered on the park bench. Meredith signed the charge, the clerk returned her credit card and cautiously boxed the crystal lighthouse.

"This will make a fine gift; a very Merry Christmas to you and your family. Do be careful. I understand the forecast is for a dangerously cold night."

The clerk's Christmas wish including family made Meredith's throat tighten. Still, she managed a heart-felt adieu, pulled the scarf over her hair and approached the door. The bell jingled her exit and she stepped from the warmth of the gift shop into the freeze and smell of winter's cold on her face, and the crunch of the frozen snow beneath her feet. She pulled the hood of her coat over her head and began the short walk to her office located diagonally across the street from the small shop.

Denver & McClain; Attorneys at Law
10 Market Square
Claremont, Tennessee

Meredith McClain's image was dwarfed by the Palladian window four stories above the snow-covered streets. Her mind was so engrossed in the afternoon's events, she was unaware of her trance, her right hand embracing her waist, her other hand fingering the strands of her hair that touched the shoulders of her wool, navy blue business suit.

Beyond the street below, on the distant horizon, the Great Smokey Mountains rose into the silver-gray sky, a giant saddlery of snow-covered topography in the early afternoon fade of winter sun. Below, Market Street teemed with shoppers moving briskly between brightly-lit shops, seemingly ignoring the falling snow. The spirit of the season was evident, shoppers slowing their pace to speak a brief 'Season's Greetings'. But Meredith's mind was on neither, the season nor the apparently warm exchange of the faith and hope the season represented. It was futile, she could not pull her mind away from the park, and the figure of the small boy child still huddled on the park bench.

Meredith failed to hear the brief knock and the opening of her office door. "Cinnamon and pine is the essence of Christmas!"

Still entranced, Meredith continued her gaze through the window. Bang! Sara Penski, also an attorney and Meredith's best friend, dropped a worn, brown, overstuffed accordion file onto the corner of Meredith's desk.

Startled, Meredith flinched, simply touching a finger to her forehead.

Sara cupped her hands, speaking into them to create a distant voice effect. "The world to Meredith, come in Meredith."

"Sara, my heart's in bad enough shape without the shock you just 'dropped on me'...literally."

Her hand on her chest, Meredith walked to her desk, slumped into the leather, button-studded executive chair as if out of breath. "My heart feels like I just finished a marathon."

In the absence of comment, Sara walked to the large Palladian windows. Falling temperatures had begun frosting oval vignettes on the window's panes. "What a view! In the evening sun it's as if the mountains are asleep beneath a white blanket."

Meredith straightened her posture. "What's the low temperature supposed to be tonight?"

Sara hugged herself, bunching the miniature poinsettia corsage pinned to the pocket of her wool, olive dress. "Burr! With the wind chill, I understand near zero. Why?"

"'Fiber Optics' annual Christmas party is this evening, I'm expected there with a gift, and a cake. Sub-zero temperatures scare me, not just for my travel, but because innocent children die on icy, winter nights, Sara."

"They always do."

Meredith raises her head briskly. "Sara! How cold!"

"You know I didn't mean it that way."

"I should hope not. This is the second, consecutive Christmas these kinds of frigid temperatures have been driven south by a rebel jet stream."

Sara's heels clacked on the worn, hardwood floor of the century-old building as she moved away from the windows. Her auburn curls bounced on the shoulders of the Christmas scarf playing around her neck and over her shoulder. With a look of melancholy, she touched the worn, voluminous accordion file on Meredith's desk, watching her finger sensitively drag across as if 'reading' it. "Here's the file on the Claremont Children's Home." She looked up, her face no longer melancholy. Her chin lifted and her eyes brightened, but her voice was sarcastic: "Parentless, placeless, and penniless."

"Poetic, but still cold, Sara, and don't tell me you didn't mean it the way you said it." Meredith relaxed back in the Presidential, high-backed swivel chair. "What happened to hope?"

"Hope is a wonderful thing, but if you think this case is going to be anything this side of sad, demoralizing, and just plain heart-wrenching, you might seriously consider upgrading that to, 'miracle'."

Meredith lifted an engaging brow as obvious dissent began morphing her face into a bellicose appearance.

Sara interrupted before Meredith could comment. "I know...how about a little faith, Sara?"

Meredith sniped back: "You're a regular doubting Thomas."

"I prefer, 'realistic', thank you. After all, these children are going to be left in the lion's den. None of them are Daniels, and Gabriel isn't going to deliver them. Whatever is required to deliver them from the jaws of these lions will require nothing less than divine intervention. Everything's against them, Meredith, even the social help agencies, not to mention the justice system."

Meredith raised her hands in frustration, and her voice dripped with sarcasm. "God forbid the 'spirit of the law' even get consideration here, Sara."

"You're the one who brought up hope."

Meredith flashed a pseudo smile. "You have forgotten part of your argument, Ms. Prosecutor. If you will recall, the Devil's angel, the Prince of Persia, captured and imprisoned Gabriel, and God sent Michael to deliver didn't he?"

Sara was silent, and Meredith matched her silence. As Meredith opened the accordion file, she was immediately distracted by a group photo of twenty-four children, an obviously joyful and smiling Meredith McClain in the midst of them, her hair windblown, the children's smiles reflecting the same warmth the bright sun added to the photo.

Meredith gazed at the photo intensely. "If I could, I'd take every single one of them home with me, Sara, assuring that each received the love and attention the heart of every child deserves."

"Tiny Tim couldn't have said it better."

"You're a regular walking, talking, library of literature, Sara."

"Thank you. However, I might add you're alliteration to be outstanding."

Sara's chuckle was sardonic. "Somehow, I...just can't wrap my mind around the vision of Brett bouncing two babies on his knees while helping 22 other children with homework, all of whom are under fourteen, I might add."

Meredith simultaneously lifted her brow and smiled. *"I can do all things through Christ Jesus which strengthenth me."* She exaggerated her smile as she curled the fore and middle fingers of both hands into quotes.

"Now we're into existential Christianity. Correct me if I'm wrong, but Brett is the problem here, and, if my memory serves me correctly, the Bible warns of the futility of self renovation and turning over new leaves. In other words, and excuse my poor English, that ain't gonna happen?"

Meredith's face brightened. "Agnostic Sara is reading the scriptures? A little 'upgrading' maybe?"

"Meredith McClain, though you're my best friend, you don't know everything about my beliefs and habits."

Meredith mused at Sara pulling a worn, leather Bible tucked snugly between two finely-crafted mallard duck bookends, seemingly skillfully flipping through its pages. "One problem is, self renovation wears old with time, ultimately yielding to forgotten commitments and promises; and we are warned about turning over new leaves, because the leaf is the same on--"

"Both sides. I know, and I believe it also says that '*...the latter end of the man is worse than the first.*'"

Meredith smiled both surprise and approval, still musing at Sara as she returned the Bible to its place between the bookends.

Sara massaged her arms with her palms. "I wouldn't have chosen the word, futile; and second...the passage just plain gives me the willies."

Meredith rose and moved around her desk. Sara backed up, as if from Meredith, falling onto the soft, leather sofa matching Meredith's executive chair. But Meredith stopped and turned, leaning against the end of her desk, casting her gaze toward the Palladian windows. "Something won't let me give up on Brett just yet. Time reveals truth, and maybe truth will reveal a Brett I have yet to know, one of faith and not doubt." She glanced visual emphasis over her shoulder toward Sara and exhaled: "The very reason I have yet to agree to, or refuse to marry him."

Meredith backed up casually, plopping down onto the sofa next to Sara, closing her eyes, pressing her palms to her forehead as if to ease a headache. "I do love him, Sara."

Sara's frown tightened, accentuated by squinted eyes. "I know you do; and because we're best friends is the only reason I say what I'm about to say, that I've wanted to say for a long time. Be realistic, Meredith; the man doesn't want children; he's totally secular, and not even receptive to the concept of faith. Worse, he's not only self-centered, but edging on egomaniacal. That's a lot of leaf-turning to ask of anyone."

Meredith opened her eyes, dropped her hands to her lap, rested her head to the back of the sofa, and turned to look at Sara, her voice almost mystic. "I can't counter any of those, Sara."

"Well, glory be. You see the light."

"But wait. *'With men it is impossible, but not with God: for with God all things are possible.'*"

Sara looked away as she rose from the sofa, her demeanor seemingly driven by both adrenalin and her skills at legal debate. "Come on, Meredith. This has nothing to do with God. You and Brett are not only different, you're nothing alike. Brett Collier is bowling, beer, and brogans while Meredith is symphony, sweet tea, and Jesus shoes. No matter how you cut it, you and Bret are the perfect amalgam."

"Point well made, counselor. Fortunately, life is not a courtroom."

Suddenly it was Sara leaning against the front of Meredith's desk. She turned, extending her hands. "Wanna bet?" Meredith rose to accept Sara's extended hands. "Meredith, you have everything a man could want: totally beautiful in mind and body, educated, a successful professional, and most importantly—Sara rolled her eyes— maybe a little prudish, but a heart of gold."

Meredith dropped Sara's hand, her gaze hostile. "Sara, above all people, you know I'm not a situational ethics person! While values are desirable, there's something more to be treasured, and that's morals; and regardless of the language, for me the translation is simple—no ring, no bed."

A quiet knock emanated from the door. Prematurely gray, Richard Gere look-alike, and senior partner, R. Samuel Denver, Esq., entered, buttoning the coat of his navy blue suit from John H. Daniels Co. "Another debate between philosopher and theologian, I assume?"

He picked up the voluminous accordion file on Meredith's desk and examined the identifying tab. "I understand there's little we can do for these folks, so go easy on the *'pro bono.'*"

Meredith laughed. "Sam, raising kids is all *'pro bono.'*"

"*Touché*. Though wittily, and not necessarily warmly, you continue to reaffirm why I made you full partner, Meredith." He looked at Sara.

"Don't look at me. I don't have a client in this suit."

Meredith's voice was haughty. "In spite of your insensitivity, we still love you, Sam. Merry Christmas."

Denver crossed the spacious office and opened the door, but paused before exiting. "You can go back to your debate now. I came in for two reasons, first, to say that I hope you both have a terrific Christmas; and second, your new cell phone could literally be a life-saver in this kind of weather, so be sure to carry it at all times. Besides, I may need you."

"Not at Christmas, Sam," Meredith and Sara responded in unison.

Samuel Denver only smiled as he eased the door closed behind him.

Meredith cast a hurried glance at her watch. "Speaking of leaving, I still have a cake to bake, a face and body to make presentable, then drive to Knoxville—all by six o'clock, I might add."

Sara's face was grim. "In this frigid weather? Meredith, what are you thinking? The weather isn't bad, it's scary bad; you have no business--"

Meredith interrupted with a 'that's not a consideration' expression. "Brett would be furious."

Sara's words dripped with sarcasm. "By all means let's not upset Brett."

Meredith didn't counter, but leaned against the desk and crossed her arms, her gaze perplexed and fixed on Sara.

Sara was defensive, starting to back toward the door. "I...think this is where I came in."

Meredith mellowed. "Don't go just yet. Let me make a couple of notes first, and you can walk me to the door."

Sara stepped forward and sat on the arm of the sofa and rested her hands in her lap. "I know you neither want, nor need a lecture, but a different perspective can help; and pardon me while I wax profound, but lasting relationships are built upon things common, not things different. I know how you met, but how you ever came to tolerate each other philosophically is beyond a mystery."

"You've obviously forgotten James Carville and Mary Matalin, happily married yet serious political and philosophical opponents."

"Exception noted."

Meredith's eyes focused on the pencil and legal pad, her hand unconsciously alternating the pencil end to end. "As you know, I met Brett when we represented Fiber Optics. It was my first big case with Denver; remember?"

"A victory everyone knows was largely due to you, I might add."

"It's nice to be reminded everyone thought so; thank you. Anyway, the suit targeted Brett's department; we worked together closely. Admittedly, there's a little pronounced ego there, but—"

"A little pronounced ego?" Sara interrupted.

Meredith ignored the interruption. "Beyond which I found a warm, kind, and honest man. He strongly defended his employees, and not just his company. Both his family and Fiber Optics supported him. After suffering the opposite, a totally bitter end of my own personal tragedy, I was impressed."

Sara straightened her posture, surprise covering her face. "Are you saying that Denver didn't back you regarding the accident?"

"Yes, but not my in-laws." Meredith rested her face in

her hands as if for support. "My father-in-law turned on me as if half-crazed. His words were not only in my face, but fierce and ugly: "'Meredith, you two weren't whiny-mouthed, pea-brained teenagers. Sledding down hills and open fields is dangerous enough, but on busy public roads is unthinkable. It eludes me how either of you could have failed to recognize the obvious danger. Did neither of you read <u>Ethan Frome</u> in your high school literature?'"

Meredith shook her head and closed her eyes. "Instantly, he developed a cold glare on his face I had never seen before. He was so angry, he was unaware he crushed the soft drink can he held. His scolding was bad, but his accusation unbearable." Meredith covered her mouth with her hand as a tear tumbled from her eye, tracking a path down her cheek. "His words still haunt me to this day."

Sara eased around the desk behind Meredith and gently stroked her hair before she eased herself onto the desk beside Meredith.

Meredith continued, tearfully. "That's when I realized the greater shock wasn't his accusation, but his admission of unbelief."

Sara shook her head in question. "His unbelief?"

Meredith looked up at Sara. "He said: 'Because of you I will see neither my son, nor my grandson ever again.'"

"I'm so sorry. I know how that must have impacted you," opined Sarah.

"On the heels of all that was the Fiber Optics lawsuit, which was major stress. But you know what? Brett never left my side through the entire ordeal. A thousand times he must have said, 'Meredith, I both believe you, and believe in you.'"

Meredith sat in silence a moment. "No, Brett doesn't want children, he is largely agnostic, and yes again, he sometimes does think too highly of himself. But he stood with me through the worst crisis in my life. I can't help but believe that a loving, caring, Brett Collier lives within the confines of all that...that...for lack of a better word, 'secular posture'. But that Brett has for some reason retreated to a place so deep inside, he is out of view." Meredith paused, her gaze serious. "He's even out of view of himself."

Meredith covered Sara's hand with hers, her words broken. "I somehow feel that even though I know I'm not responsible, I've failed him in not finding out why, thus, I am uncomfortable judging him."

The intercom buzzed. "Miss McClain, Mr. Collier is on line one."

Sara slid off the desk. "Speaking of the Devil."

Meredith pushed the intercom button. "Tell him I just left," she replied, and watched until the call light was extinguished.

Sara gave Meredith an approving nod.

Meredith removed her charcoal winter coat and scarf

from the coat tree's brass head. "Give me a call over the holidays and we'll do lunch, provided the weather cooperates."

"Lunch may be the only way of getting your present to you."

Meredith and Sara left the office and wound their way down the professionally decorated staircase and into the spacious lobby. Momentarily they admired the 12-foot spruce pine that had transformed the cold, open, two-story glass vestibule into a presentation of Christmas warmth. Meredith had no more than wrapped the green and red scarf snugly about her neck and pulled the collar of her wool coat tight than she turned, crossed the vestibule and started up the stairs.

"What did you forget?"

"I'll tell you," Meredith said, disappearing up the stairs.

Meredith returned to the front door. "What did you forget?" Sara asked.

"Without this I might as well not show up at Brett's Christmas party this evening. It's our gift for the President of Fiber Optics, Inc., and his wife."

"Oh my, can anything else be as important?"

Sara opened the door to the invading cold air that blew winter frowns onto their faces while parting their hair.

"Geez, it's freezing, Meredith. Be sure and let Brett

know the exact time you leave so he will know when to expect you."

The two women embraced. "I will, and Merry Christmas, Sara."

"You, too, Meredith."

Meredith stepped onto the snowy walk at a cautious pace. Just beyond 'Class is Glass', she prepared to see if the boy was still in the park, hoping he would be gone, and that his mother had returned for him. But she was distracted by an approaching troupe of youthful madrigal singers from her church.

"Merry Christmas, Ms. McClain."

"Thank you. A Merry Christmas to all of you."

The troupe of singers carried donation canisters. As Meredith made a charitable donation, her mobile phone rang. In September, Denver and Meredith had added the newest model, the 'Smartphone'. With the new PDA feather, Meredith had her on 'personal digital assistant'.

"Hello."

"I called your apartment. Thought you were leaving early today?"

Meredith frowned at the arctic-like air that blasted her face. "I had to pick up a hostess gift, something I want Harrison and Maggie to appreciate as well as enjoy. I told you I would be on time, Brett."

"No problem; just checking. But you know how much

this annual event means to me."

"I'll be there, and on time," Meredith screeched, her throat tightened by both temperature and frustration. "I'm cold, Brett; I need to go."

"Okay, stay in touch."

Meredith closed the phone, pushing it into the side pocket of her black, leather attaché. Pulling up her hood, she secured the box containing her cherished purchase. "Sometimes I not only think, but believe he cares more for that job and Fiber Optics than for me," she said aloud.

Meredith arrived at the park, immediately noting the bench was empty. Since the clerk at the glass shop had reported that the boy had faithfully warmed himself in the shop, she hurried back to look through the window to see if the boy was in the shop. He was.

"Oh dear; that boy's mother hasn't come for him yet. If could get my hands on her, I think I would choke her," Meredith argued to herself. "At least he's in the shop, but he won't have that shelter after they close."

Patiently, she waited at the curb for a snow-covered vehicle to creep past her through the slush of snow. She crossed the street and entered the foyer of the 19th Century, stone, Victorian Building, unlocked her mailbox and retrieved the contents before mounting the steep staircase that lead to her rooftop apartment. Once inside the apartment, she removed her coat, moved to the fireplace, turned the gas knob and the fireplace logs ignited with a swish. She selected the "*Songs of the Season*" channel on the TV and momentarily the drum rolls of "The Little Drummer Boy" began.

Meredith struck a long-stemmed match from the ornate canister and odors of sulfur pinched the air. She lit the two large, red, designer candles that occupied opposite ends of the white, wooden-mantled fireplace and a cinnamon fragrance filled the room. Centered on the mantle was a gilded framed photo of Meredith, her handsome husband, Richard, and between them, their six year old son, Richie. The warm, brown eyes and bright smile of the boy in the photo instantly stole the viewer's attention. All were dressed in white, all smiled, and all were obviously happy. Next to the photo of Meredith's parents was a small, wooden train made from yellow poplar, hand-carved by Meredith's late father for his only grandson, Richie. She was overwhelmed; tears formed in her eyes and her throat tightened, so much so, her words, "God give me grace" were hardly audible.

She pulled a tissue from a box on the end table. As she blotted her damp cheeks, she engaged the foot switch that lit the large, professionally-decorated Christmas tree that centered the wreathed, glass wall of Palladian windows. Overlooking the icy street below, the windows provided a panoramic, unobstructed view into the park beyond that had been transformed into a snowy, winter wonderland. The boy's absence on the park bench somewhat alleviated her concerns. "Thank you, Lord. Either his mother has come for him after all, or he's still in the store."

The phone rang.

"Hello."

Brett's voice was the tone of a commander in a briefing. "I forgot to tell you to bring my day planner; it's on the foyer table." His voice mellowed. "And what award-winning cake is my beautiful 'flower of jurisprudence' preparing for this evening?"

"I'm not superstitious, but I think maybe my favorite."

"And that is?"

"King's Cake."

"What's that?"

"It's a cake with hidden treasure inside."

"Really? And just what might be the treasure?"

"Chocolate coins covered with gold foil. The pieces of cake containing the coins will provide good fortune in the new year for those getting those pieces of cake."

"You always come through with something unique as well as delicious. This weather's getting nasty, so be careful. Oh, and don't forget my planner, and don't...."

"I know, Brett. Don't be late."

The oven preheated while Meredith gathered the

ingredients for the cake she hoped would repeat her much lauded success of the previous Christmas. She took a coffee can from the cabinet, dipped the coffee into the old percolator that had belonged to Meredith's mother.

"Adding an extra scoop will hopefully help me endure one more demanding call from Brett," she said audibly.

The strange, unexpected sensation that had drawn her to the window at the gift shop suddenly gripped her again. She went to the windows but paused a moment, hoping that when she looked down on the park, the boy would be gone. But that wasn't the view Meredith had hoped for. The boy's return to the park bench proved the stir of her spirit to be accurate, and anticipation squeezed into an uncomfortable lump in her throat. "Something's not right here, and if someone doesn't take control of the situation, that child is going to freeze to death."

Meredith turned down the oven slightly, hurried across the massive apartment, and from the closet pulled on her wool, winter coat. She descended the long staircase, hurried through the foyer and onto the icy sidewalk, cautiously crossing the street to the park. She broke her hurry to a walk so as not to startle the boy. She nonchalantly approached the snow-huddled figure on the bench.

"Hello. May I sit beside you?"

The boy didn't reply, simply dusted the snow from the

bench beside him.

"Thank you! That's gentlemanly of you. My name is Meredith. I had a little boy once. What's your name, and how old you are?"

Again the boy failed to reply, and Meredith repeated the question. Though the boy didn't reply again, his body jerked and shivered almost in a rhythm. His voice emerged from a face that peeped through the hood of a shabby, denim coat. "Jonah, and I'm twelve," he said curtly.

"It's terribly cold out here, Jonah. My apartment is just across street, and it's really snug and warm. Why don't you come over and...."

"I can't; my Mom's comin' for me."

"I'm very glad to hear that, Jonah."

His eyes followed Meredith's finger as she pointed. "See those large windows on the top floor of that building? That's my apartment. You could watch for your mom while staying warm all at the same time. With the size of those windows you couldn't possibly miss her."

Jonah abruptly stood. "No. I have to wait here."

Meredith stood as well, presenting herself as a professional before she thought. "Jonah, I could call the police, and they would come pick you up, and by no choice of your own. It's going to be deadly cold this evening, so they would take you to a safe shelter. The temperature is going to dip below zero; you could freeze."

"I won't freeze; my mother will come; she promised."

Meredith thought to herself: "Well, you blew that one, Meredith." She thought for a quick few second. "I tell you what. Let's make a deal. I won't call the police, but only under one condition."

The pubescent boy scowled at Meredith, but not with total rejection. When a sudden gust of wind felt like a knife slicing Meredith's face, she knew she must do something, and now.

Normally, she would have called the police, and without question or hesitation. However, her mind searched frantically for something she could offer for her 'conditional' agreement. "Lord, help me," she prayed to herself.

"Okay, Jonah, here's the deal. If you will keep warming yourself in the gift shop every few minutes, I will bring you fresh hot chocolate until your mother arrives. But if she hasn't shown up by the time the gift shop closes, you must promise to come to my apartment. We can leave a note on the bench telling your mother exactly where you are, and that we are watching for her from the tall windows."

For reassurance, Meredith again pointed to the large Palladian windows in her loft apartment. "If for some reason she doesn't come by tomorrow morning, then I will help you find your mother. You see, I'm a lawyer with a special interest in children, and I know about these things.

Deal?"

"You are?" Retreating, Jonah stepped backwards, rejecting Meredith's extended, black leather-gloved hand. It concerned Meredith that a 12 year old boy reacted negatively to her being an attorney.

"Okay. But my mother will come. You'll see. She'll come."

Fifteen minutes later, Meredith had restarted the process, checked the status of her cake and prepared fresh hot chocolate for Jonah. Cautiously, she again crossed the street into the park, handing Jonah the cup of Hot Chocolate as promised. The boy began drinking the hot liquid instantly.

"Be careful! It's hot and could burn you."

"It's very good. Thank you."

At least for the moment, with mission accomplished, Meredith returned to her apartment.

Meredith's heart was wrenched in anguish as she looked down from her own tower of security and warmth, watching Jonah sip the hot chocolate as he fidgeted on the bench, obviously to keep warm. Even in the warmth of her apartment, between thoughts of the boy on the bench and the threatening temperatures, chill bumps easily and freely ran the length of her body. She stepped out of her ankle-high boots only to have her feet attacked by the icy water from the snow melted from her boots. "I didn't even think about his feet. I bet he doesn't have on boots."

In a priority to hurry to observe Jonah from the window, she had forgotten to leave her boots in the foyer. She removed her wet socks, laid them on the hearth of the fireplace to dry, and went to the bureau in her bedroom for dry socks.

A Christmas tree ornament unexpectedly pinged a quick refrain of <u>Silent Night</u>, and Meredith did something she hadn't wanted to do—press the talk button on the phone and dial.

"Police Department; Officer Jacobs speaking. May I help you?"

"Jake. Meredith. Call me."

She hung up, and almost immediately the phone rang.

"Meredith, when you tell me to call you, that signals privacy needed; what's up?"

"Thanks for the quick call back, Jake. Well, after changing out of wet socks a moment ago--"

"Why do I have a feeling that wet socks are in someway related to the reason for this call?"

"Skip the melodrama, Jake. I have what I think is a potentially serious problem that may require your help, and I need your word that this is between us only."

"You got it."

"Has a missing person report been filed on a twelve-year-old-boy within the last twenty-four hours?"

"Not that I'm aware of, but I just came on duty, so let me check for any postings."

Meredith listened to the rustle of papers, footsteps on a hard floor, then the voice of Jacobs again. "Nothing on anyone remotely close to anyone age twelve."

Meredith began, but Jake interrupted.

"Though I'm on my cell, I think I need to step into the hallway so I won't be heard. Hang on a second."

Meredith heard Jake's movements; a door opened and closed. "Okay"

Meredith related the facts of the story, then her suspicions.

"Meredith, if this is what I think you're suggesting, it has disaster written all over it. Let Children's Services handle this. You don't need to get involve--"

"Jake, at this point I'm not suggesting anything, just trying to figure out what's going on here. My gut feeling is telling me something is wrong beyond the child himself."

"What did you have for lunch that has so upset you?"

"Jake, please. I'm serious."

"Okay, if the boy will cooperate follow through with your plan. But, keep it to yourself, and if the boy's mother doesn't show in the next eighteen hours, I'll step in. As you know, if I become involved, that automatically includes Children's Services"

Meredith sighed. "I know, and all too well. Thanks,

Jake.   You're a good friend, and not just to me, but humanity at large."

"I'd rather be the man of your dreams."

Meredith sighed. "I know, and I'm probably blind."

"Say goodnight, Meredith."

"Goodnight, Jake."

With the cake's layers complete, Meredith again decided the King's Cake was the correct choice for Brett's Christmas party and continued the preparation. Completing the cake, running back and forth to the window, agonizing over the heart-wrenching scene unfolding in the icy park below, and keeping Jonah supplied with hot chocolate had been challenging, to say the least.

The afternoon waned and Meredith faced not only the probable chance of being late at the Fiber Optics party, but a possibility of being absent. Worse, she would not only have to explain to Brett, but to his boss, Harrison, and his wife, Maggie.

The clock seemed to glare at Meredith and the second hand seemingly pulsated its rhythm in her ear as Meredith began the process of salvaging the disaster she saw to be all but imminent. "Though belated, maybe the beautiful, Steinbach crystal will somehow make up for my absence," she said, leaning her palms on the kitchenette table, perplexed.

With the close proximity of the courthouse, the five

o'clock chimes were clear and distinct, heavy with the burden of the moment.

Meredith returned to the windows only to discover Jonah running toward the gift shop. She picked up the binoculars she kept on the window sills for bird watching, or any other situation needing acuity or a closer view. From her vantage point high above the park, she saw the 'closed' sign was now in the shop's door window, and except for the display lights, the shop was dark. Jonah was trying the door. Frantically he then ran from the door to the windows, but to no avail.

Meredith agonized with Jonah's every step as he slowly straggled back to the snowy bench with his shoulders slumped in defeat. This time, in addition to the lump in her throat, Meredith felt an alarm-like squeeze in her chest, and an elephant-like weight that heart attack victims often describe. Especially disconcerting was the defeated bow of his head and slump of his shoulders as he laid down on the bench. Sheer panic roared through Meredith's being as she helplessly tapped at the pane of her window, failing to reason the tap on the windows impossible to hear at that distance not even a consideration. But then, that's the response of the autonomic reaction to panic.

"No! No! Jonah, you can't go to sleep; you'll freeze," Meredith cried. But only the window could hear.

Meredith was jerked into even a deeper reality when

an intermittent, irritating, sound scratched from the television, followed by the announcement: *"This is the National Weather Service in Morristown, Tennessee. Increasing snow and sub-zero temperatures are expected tonight..."*

The remainder of the severe weather warning Meredith did not hear as she clutched her face in her palms. "This can't wait; I have to do this, and I have to do it now."

In seconds she was again in her winter coat, hurrying down the stairs and cautiously traversing the icy street to the park. She was unable to avert the wave of icy slush that sprayed her from a passing vehicle. Nonetheless, she trudged forward. She lifted Jonah from his prone position on the bench. His face and ears was a thermometer red, his eyes watery, and he appeared almost incoherent. His denim coat and gloves were totally inadequate for the sub-normal temperature. Meredith wrapped him in her own winter coat. She knew that with her thin, five-foot-four inch frame, if Jonah didn't cooperate, carrying him would be physically impossible.

"Jonah, we have to get you inside. You're a big boy, and I will need your help."

"No!" he shouted, trying to again lie down on the bench. "My mother will be here."

Meredith bit her lip, then matched Jonah's rebuke. "Jonah! Listen to me! Shall I call the police?"

When he failed to respond, she pulled him to her; this time he offered no resistance, verbal or physical. Subconsciously, Meredith was gripped in the memory of her own inabilities to affect the accident that had taken the life of her own young son, and cannot help crying as she sternly admonishes Jonah: "I can't carry you; you will have to help. Please!"

Looking into Meredith's face, Jonah rose from the bench, moving his arm around Meredith's waist.

With the lapse of time between the splash of the passing vehicle, persuading Jonah to come with her, and their trek out of the park, Meredith's wet clothing had itself become a threat, her body all but numb.

In the foyer of the building her knees buckled, and she and Jonah both crash onto the cold, wooden steps. She knew her legs weren't numb by the excruciating pains that radiated not only up her legs, but by the extended burning sensation penetrating her torso. She could also no longer resist the agony reverberating in her body. Like an injured animal, she howled her pain aloud. However, sensing Jonah's assistance, she re-engaged her effort to get them up the stairs. At the door she was challenged yet again. Her hands were so cold she couldn't turn the knob. As if reading her thoughts, Jonah twisted the knob and the door opened. The immediate difference in temperature was nothing less than a dual burst of both the much needed energy and hope.

"I'll turn the fire up, Jonah."

Surprisingly, Meredith could actually feel her hand grip the lever as she turned on the gas logs. Between breaths of warmth blown onto her fingers, she told Jonah what to do. "The bathroom is in the hallway, towels are in the closet. Strip off your clothes, dry your body, make absolutely sure you are dry, then wrap yourself in the towel and come to the fireplace. I'll have a quilt ready, and while you sit in front of the fire and warm, I'll make you some hot chicken soup."

While Jonah was in the bathroom, Meredith went to the kitchen, opened two cans of chicken soup and dumped the contents into a sauce pan. She heard Jonah in the living room. "Are you in front of the fire?"

"Yes."

"Don't get too close; I'll bring a quilt in a second."

She took one of her grandmother's patch quilts from the hall closet. Swaddling Jonah in the worn quilt activated the odor of moth balls, which sprang memories to her mind of her grandmother swaddling her in the quilt, pushing her loving, arthritic fingers through her granddaughter's hair.

Like his clothing, Jonah's body was dirty. She had not allowed her thoughts to become audible but to herself: "I can't imagine how long it's been since his golden hair and blue eyes have peeped from beneath the scum on his body."

She gently took Jonah's face in her hands. "You just snuggle into this quilt while I finish your soup."

Meredith returned to the kitchen and sampled the soup. "Not yet."

In her bathroom, for her own pain she swallowed four Ibuprofen tablets, half of a full day's dosage and stripped herself of the wet clothes she had forgotten she wore. She toweled herself dry, got into fresh underclothing, and into her magnolia winter robe that felt like it had the weight of one of her grandmother's home made comforters.

After Jonah finally submitted to the unwanted shower, Meredith unfolded mahogany accent tables in front of the Palladian windows, setting Christmas place mats, napkins, bowls, and flatware. With the exception of her knees, her body pain had somewhat subsided. Her attention focused purely on Jonah, however, with relief as he gobbled down a second bowl of the hot chicken soup.

In fades of faint orange and magenta, sunset peeped through broken shards of the gray, western sky. Jonah looked at Meredith, his expression forlorn, his sigh a sad confessional. "She's not coming, is she?"

Surprised at the reversal in his confidence, and the empathy that burned within her, Meredith felt Jonah just may now allow her to take him in her arms. Her cautious reach for him was, however, interrupted by the phone's ring. Knowing it was Brett, and that her failure to answer would only suggest that she may have driven into a ditch or had an accident mandated she answer the phone, which she did, but with reluctance.

"Meredith, where are you?"

She allowed the disappointing interruption of tending to Jonah to anger her. "What a time to call, Brett. Hang on a minute."

Brett's antagonistic tone and arousal of her own anger drove Meredith to her bedroom for privacy. "Okay, I'm back."

"It's six o'clock. Where in God's name are you? I left a message--"

"Brett, I'd prefer you calling on God with a more legitimate plea, and incidentally, in whose name I'm trying to remedy the situation I have on my hands. But to answer your question, I've been out, and I'm very busy."

"You've been out? Busy with the cake I should hope."

"Brett, I have an emergency here, and to be honest, it's not the cake."

His tone changed from condescending to almost alarm: "What kind of emergency."

"A twelve-year-old-boy has waited for hours in the park in this horrific weather for a mother who's failed to show, even to this moment. He's fortunate not to have frostbite. Worse, he had no place to go, so I brought him to my apartment."

Brett's forced exhale was so audible, Meredith couldn't determine if his voice resonated with disappointment or anger. "Meredith. Meredith. Have you lost your mind? For God's sake call the police. Oh, sorry for the frivolous use of the God word. Let Children's Service take him to a shelter where he can be safely boarded until they find his mother."

Meredith's lip quivered, her whole physiology seemingly involuntarily manifesting its anger it its own way. Remembering her dear grandmother's expression in such situations, she repeated her prayer: "Dear God, do help me to be a Christian in these days of trial, tribulation, and turmoil."

"Brett! I'll have you know I have been a mother, and I know perfectly well a child's needs, and proper care. Children need love, not rejection, especially at Christmas, and especially not in some non-personal atmosphere when they can be in a real and loving home."

"Meredith, you know how you impressed Harrison and Maggie last year. He's anticipating another 'culinary extraordinaire.'" Brett's voice brightened. "In all probability, a vice-presidency is at our fingertips."

Meredith remained silent so as not to display that she had gone from anger to livid outrage, now noted in her extended silence.

"Meredith, this is my job, my future."

"Brett, if you believe your future hangs on a piece of cake, you need help, and more than psychological help."

Brett laughed, and with a haughty air. "Don't start the religious stuff, Meredith."

"Brett Collier, if I could get a hold of you right now, I'd...I'd..."

"You'd what, act even more childish?"

Now furious, she knew she couldn't answer sanely and without sinning against herself.

Her extended silence yet again had pushed Brett to the point his voice leapt beyond serious to threat: "I'm only going to ask once more."

Meredith shook her head. "Did you just give me an ultimatum?"

"What should you expect--"

Meredith's anger bowled over, boiling from her chest to her mouth and from the end of her tongue. "I've been to your so-called 'Christmas parties.' A child's welfare is more important than some drunken dinner party that represents anything but Christmas. Now if you want to spend Christmas with real people dealing with the real world celebrating the real meaning of Christmas, you're welcome here. Otherwise, stay where you are. Merry Christmas, Brett!"

In actuality, the lump that had not left Meredith's throat since discovering Jonah in the park, now drove an expanded pain, that in her heart. Unlike that for Jonah, this pain now choked her.

She refused to cry until she was off the phone. The instant she returned the phone to its cradle, she collapsed onto the bed's cream and mocha-checked comforter, sobbing. Moments later she felt the gentle touch of a small hand on her arm. She looked up and into Jonah's warm, brown eyes. Wiping her own tears, she conjured up a smile while rustling his blonde hair. "It may be suppertime, but how about you and I having breakfast?" she asked as her voice broke.

Jonah's eyes brightened. Through blurred vision, Meredith realized that the boy reaching out to comfort her was also smiling for the first time.

Meredith oiled a pan, chopped onions, green peppers, chilies, mushrooms, cubed ham, and last, cilantro, spiking the kitchen with enticing aromas. After whipping eggs with a little milk, Meredith soon turned Christmas colored omelets onto hand-painted Christmas china. Watching a hungry Jonah cram the warm food into his mouth and gulp milk from the gold-rimmed matching Christmas goblets provided yet another unwanted suggestion...that Jonah had gone hungry. The warm sensation in her breast that only a mother's love can prompt, reminded her of the huge void that the loss of her only son had left in her heart and life.

She felt a renewed energy, even regenerated a sense

of humor. "Hungry little critter aren't you?"

"Yeah."

Again, the discipline of motherly instincts nudged her. "You mean, 'yes ma'am' don't you?

"Sorry. Yes Ma'am."

Jonah started to wipe his mouth on his sleeve, but Meredith stopped his arm, handing him the cloth, Christmas napkin pulled from its wooden nutcracker ring garnished with chestnut and garland. "A napkin works much better."

Jonah wiped his mouth more like it was a 'deep cleaning' process than simply removing food from his mouth. His hunger now abated, he strolled to the large Palladian windows, his eyes scanning the park below that was gradually being rapidly swallowed by night.

A mere bead of burnt orange marked the horizon like the thin line of an all but closed eye. In the park, the snow-covered gazebo, arbor, and swing sat still and quiet. But that evening, the simple bench was the park's centerpiece. In the fade of twilight, a snow-sprinkled, red Christmas bow with green garland glistened from the park's gas lamp that lit the park bench, circling a amber hue on the blanket of virgin snow. Jonah seemed to hide his face in his arms, resting them on the window sill.

Meredith massaged Jonah's back with a slow, gentle, circular motion. "Want to tell me about your mother and your family?"

Jonah remained silent. Slowly moving from beneath Meredith's hands seemed more like hard labor, the drape of his arms to his side, lifeless as he all but stumbled across the floor until he dropped onto the overstuffed, earth-tone sofa.

The sharp squeeze if the pain again swelled in Meredith's chest. She escaped to the kitchen to spare Jonah seeing or hearing her cry. At the kitchen counter she rested her head on her arms, her face in her hands. In her mind, the arms of her own son reluctantly yielded their lock around her neck as she tucked him in. Griping and vivid were his words: "Goodnight, Mommy."

The scene in her mind was such that her attempt at muffling her cries was as difficult as trying to stop an ever-sickened stomach from the ever intensifying convulsions that would inevitably empty it of its contents.

She escaped to the bathroom, but her nausea was overcome with the words: "Lord, what more will you ask of me?"

Minutes later she stared in the bathroom mirror at the pale, mascara-streaked face, the warm washcloth erasing the black bleed from her cheeks, and the push of the brush through her hair restored an acceptable appearance before returning to the living room.

The figure of the boy more adolescent than pubescent slept quietly and peacefully on the sofa. She covered him with the patch quilt, dimmed the lights, and lowered the volume of the seasonal music playing on the TV. She relaxed on the sofa, gently moving Jonah's legs across her lap and relaxed her head onto the back of the sofa.

Meredith was awakened by mumbled words. "Leave her alone, Leo. Mom, stop letting him hit you." Awakened and startled by his own scuffling, Jonah sat up, his eyes wide with fright.

Attempting to recover from her own sudden awakening, Meredith instinctively snuggled Jonah's head to her breasts. "It's all right, Jonah. It's only a bad dream. Mommy is here." She immediately recognized her error in identifying herself as the boy's mother. But Jonah's cling to her only tightened, his return of her affection a welcomed surprise.   Reminded of her own little Richie, Meredith squinted, tightly shutting her eyes to hold back the possibility of tears overflowing her eyes. She pulled Jonah more firmly into her arms as she prayed to herself. "Thank you, Lord, but don't...."

Jonah's whimper interrupted her silent prayer.

"Meredith is here, Jonah. Go back to sleep."

With the room's soft lights, melodic Christmas carols, and the fire's flames licking shadowed ballerinas on the apartment walls, it was a opera of peace, love, and hope.

The music changed, Jonah's eyes opened, relaxed and warm, fixed on Meredith as she quietly sang along in her contralto, Karen Carpenter-like voice. *"O little town of Bethlehem, how still we see thee lie. Above thy deep and dreamless sleep..."* Confident, safe, and secure, Jonah's eyes lazily yielded to slumber, and his breathing to the rhythm of sleep.

Apart from Jonah's larger size, to Meredith it was much like holding her own son, Richie. She kissed Jonah's hair, again relaxing her head onto the back of the sofa with Jonah clutched gently in her arms.

A phone's distant ring rallied Meredith sufficiently that she realized the ring was not a dream. Gently slipping Jonah's body out of her embrace and onto the sofa, she hurried to her bedroom, anxious to receive what she is sure to be Brett's call of apology.

"It's about time you--"

"It's nice having someone anticipate one's call," Jake's voice interrupted.

"Sorry. I thought you were Brett. What time is it?"

"It's half past midnight; about the boy; only moments ago we received an anonymous call reporting a missing child, but we couldn't keep them on the phone long enough to trace the call."

"At least that's something, Jake. With the passing of each hour it becomes more apparent that this is more than simply a child left alone in a park."

Officer Jacobs almost plead his reply. "Meredith, it's also apparent you're becoming personally involved. I told you he needs to be in a--"

"Don't go there, Jake; not tonight, please. The office is closed for Christmas, so I'm free to devote my time to Jonah. I'll put together something of a gift for him, and if—and that's a big if, mind you—his mother through some miracle happens to show up at the park, we'll go from there."

"You're a good woman, Meredith McClain. The world needs more like you."

"You're sweet, Jake. We need more like you, too."

"Why don't we just start a mutual admiration society?"

Meredith chuckled.

"It's good to hear you laugh, Meredith."

"I owe you, Jake."

"Big time, and don't you forget it. Twelve hours remain, Meredith; that's our deal."

With her mind still roaming somewhere between semi-awake and the conversation with Jake, the call to check on Jonah, and the sleep awaiting her in the living room, Meredith returned the phone to its base. Easing the bedroom door to a silent close, in the almost hypnotic flickering shadows of the fire, she leaned against the door casing, her mind totally entranced with the lad sleeping peacefully on the sofa. One by one she extinguished the mantle's candles, the process interrupted by the sight of the hand-carved, wooden train perched on the mantle's end. Memories of her little Richie returned, he, playing with the same small train in the floor with his father.

Meredith bit her lip, attempting to restrain her heart from audibly mourning the loss of life's most precious possessions, her only son and her husband. She fought her emotions as she cautiously pushed the cherished antique train into a red box with green ribbon. Unable to find a gift label, she wrote on the back of a business card: "To Jonah with love,

From Richie."

Part

A Christmas Concerto

Meredith had set the timer on the coffee pot the previous evening as she prepared the fresh brew that co-worker Sara Penski described as 'stout.' Like an invisible ghost, Meredith's coffee not only complied with the 'law of liquids and gases', that they take the shape of their container', but moved with an aromatic virulence throughout the apartment and into Meredith's bedroom. Even so, Meredith had not lifted her head from the pillow because of the phenomenal aroma but instantly migrated to Jonah, almost as if he not even moved on the living room sofa.

In the kitchen, Meredith poured herself a cup of the fresh, strong brew. Assured Jonah still slept soundly, she returned to her bedroom, showered, and donned a white oxford blouse, denim jeans, and heavy winter socks. To her surprise, reentering the living room she discovered Jonah was dressed and had continued his vigil at the windows, viewing the sun-filled park far below and across the street.

"Good morning, Jonah."

Jonah was silent, his gaze through the huge windows unbroken. Meredith had forgotten the previous night's excruciating experience on the hard and cold stairway and knelt by the tree.

"Oh, my knees", she cried, quickly standing to hopefully arrest the pain that felt like she had touched her knee to an old 12 volt, direct current coil, which had, at least what was felt to be, twice the jolt of an equivalent in alternating current. Nonetheless, she succeeded at joyfully declaring: "Look, Jonah, there a gift is under the tree for you."

At least momentarily, the park below was unable to hold Jonah's attention over the iridescent red box tied with a brilliant green ribbon now held in Meredith's hand.

"it's really for me?"

"Are there any other Jonahs present?" Meredith called, her free hand cupped at her mouth.

She rustled Jonah's 'morning hair.' "You look like a squirrel," she said, laughing as Jonah ripped open the package. At first sight of the train, for a moment he was hesitant, his expression unbelieving.

"I know it's for a much younger boy, Jonah, but–"

"No. It's cool. It looks home made." He all but seized the business card, read it, and looked at Meredith with warm, understanding eyes. "The picture on the mantle…it belonged to him, didn't it?"

"Yes, Jonah, but now it belongs to you."

"But why doesn't it belong to him anymore? Where is

he?"

Meredith could hardly breathe, let alone speak. "Both, he and his father have gone to heaven, Jonah, where they are in wonderful, loving hands. He would want you to have it. My father carved it for Richie before he could even walk."

"That was his name, Richie?"

"Yes. Richie would sit in the floor, laughing as his father turned the train in every direction."

The door bell rang.

"Brett," Meredith chirped, jumping to her feet. Hurrying to the door, she suddenly remembered she was supposed to be angry, and delayed opening the door until she had cleared her face of anything suggesting otherwise. While her greatest hesitation was because of Brett's selfish insensitivity the previous evening, out of his mouth had come several issues that would have to be resolved before their relationship could ever have hope of return to the same footing it had previously enjoyed.

"I can't let him off too easy," she thought. She looked in the foyer mirror to assure she had killed any semblance of excitement in feeling or appearance, and put on the seasoned professional demeanor that her professional training, time, and raw, courtroom experience had taught her. She inhaled deeply, and slowly opened the door.

The slim and handsome stature of Brett Collier stood

at the door, his blue eyes a still quiet, his mouth wearing the apologetic smile she anticipated. She was, however, totally non-expectant of the arms full of gifts he carried. Her greeting was nonchalant.

"Oh, it's you, Brett."

Brett's expression was confused, and his voice almost that of a disappointed child. "May I ask whom else you were expecting?"

"After last night, it certainly wasn't you."

"Okay, I deserved that," he said. Even in the inside hallway of the building, his words atomized in the frigid air. "Meredith, it's freezing. May I--"

"How apropos for such a cold, steel heart," she thought. Stepping aside, her hand waved a silent welcome.

Jonah played with the small train, not on the floor, but on the sills of the large windows that overlooked the park, still determined to faithfully and expectantly watch for his mother.

"So this is our emergency?" Brett declared, alternating his glance between Jonah and the Christmas tree as he gingerly delivered each gift to a place beneath the tree.

"Jonah, this is Mr. Brett Collier, my fiancé. Brett, meet Jonah."

Brett smiled widely, extending his hand with expectance. "Merry Christmas, Jonah."

Jonah looked at Meredith for both, approval and confidence. She nodded affirmatively and Jonah took Brett's hand, but failed to return the smile.

Bret hung his camel, cashmere coat in the foyer closet, returned to the fireplace and rolled the sleeves of his red and black-checked flannel shirt one cuff. Warming his hands before the fire, he winked at Meredith while directing his words to Jonah. "You know what, Jonah? All these gifts can't possibly be for Meredith and me only."

Meredith's expression curled into uncertainty as she took a red Santa cap from the closet and pulled it onto Brett's head. Her raised brow and widened eyes said she was playing along. "Now you're officially, Santa."

Brett touched his still youthfully flat stomach as if it was the typically huge Santa belly, belching a Ho! Ho! Ho!' that was embarrassingly unlike the deep, resonating voice expected of Santa. "Let's see just exactly what is for whom beneath this beautiful Christmas tree" Miss Meredith has decorated.

"I would love to take credit, Jonah, but it was professionally decorated."

Brett selected a package. "Well, imagine that, it's for you, Jonah."

"Me?" Jonah surprise was surpassed only by his smile and the gleam in his eyes. He ripped off the paper and opened the box.

"Wow! a real, leather baseball glove. He fit the glove to his hand."

"Drive your fist into it several times to make a pocket," Brett instructed. Jonah responded, driving his fist into the glove's pocket several times as Brett suggested. Three loud thuds followed.

Meredith was surprised, but nonetheless elated that most all the remaining gifts were Jonah's as well. She derived deep satisfaction from the fact that Jonah's screeches of "yeah," and "all right," were evidences that he had, at least for the moment, forgotten his plight.

Brett and Jonah did a 'high five'. As Brett turned away from the tree, Jonah remarked: "But there are more gifts."

"Those are for Meredith and me. We've had a terrific Christmas just seeing you open yours for now."

Jonah was insistent. "No, everyone opens their gifts or it isn't really Christmas."

His smile was so unabashedly innocent and sincere, Meredith agreed, "Why not?"

"We should've known that. See there Jonah, you've contributed in several ways of making this an even better Christmas.

Brett tried on Meredith's gift of an expensive, suede, smoking jacket. Meredith then modeled Brett's gift of a green and red wool scarf, tam, and matching gloves.

Jonah picked up the ball glove. "You both look cool,"

he said, again sinking his fist into the pocket of the glove several times.

Meredith ripped the paper from a gift; her face beamed at the leather Bible and Bible Search software package. "Wow! I've been wanting a wide margin Cambridge and software for a long time. No more plundering through heavy, hardback concordances."

Jonah returned to enjoying his gifts. Though Meredith would have liked to, she resisted at successfully disallowing her arm to slide around Brett's waist, but not without his notice.

"Go ahead. I'd like that," he said.

Meredith ignored his approval, asking: "All these presents. Where? How? I mean––"

Unlike Meredith, Brett followed through with the slide of his arm around Meredith's waist. "We Fiber Optics of America employees may become a little over-devoted, even a little carried away at our parties, but never let it be said that we allow anything to negate our charity and generosity."

With his finger, Brett lifted Meredith's chin and looked into her eyes. "After the explanation of your unselfish absence last night, I knew I had been the perfect heel. When I explained your absence, everyone not only applauded, but insisted we create a special Christmas package for Jonah from our already-substantial collections for charity and benevolence. Well, that only made me feel the worse. That's when they also insisted making it personal by wrapping them ourselves. Everyone agreed that would make the event personal and special, and that each one could feel they were a part. At the moment I actually wondered why the party 'came to new life'. Of course it was because the party had become one of benevolence, exactly what Christmas is all about. As you had so rightly observed, I had allowed Christmas to become all about me, myself, and I rather than others. Thanks to you, the annual Fiber Optics Christmas Party had instead, become a gathering, and turned from honoring self to honoring others."

"That was very thoughtful and worthy...."

Brett quieted Meredith's lips with his finger. "But there's still something even more important. Being among all those people, I realized for the first time that being in a crowd absent the person you love, represented the loneliest place in the world. While I thought I had the most important world around me last night, your absence downgraded its importance to all but trivial. You are my world, Meredith."

Speechless and overwhelmed with both shock and joy, Meredith buried her face in the cleft of Brett's neck. "I don't know what to say."

Brett's voice was shaky, his words a little broken. "When you turned my own words on me, and asked if I was giving you an ultimatum, realizing that was precisely what I had done, it was like getting a cold glass of water in my face, and I got over both my anger and ego real fast. I wasn't only embarrassed, but instantly awakened to the fact of just how small I was even in my own eyes, and how seriously I had underestimated the quality of the person I had fallen in love with."

Jonah was again at Meredith's side, holding a gold box, a miniature green wreath centered on the box. "We forgot this tiny one."

"It's probably yours, Jonah," she said, returning her arms around Brett's neck.

Jonah held up the box to Meredith. "It says it's to you from Brett."

Still in doubt, Meredith looked down, examining the label. "Well, it looks like you're right, Jonah."

Brett's voice came from the foyer: "Meredith, you said my planner was on the foyer table, but I don't see it."

After last night's uproar over the planner, and today's display of love, remorse, and true repentance, Meredith was shocked, even unsure of what she had just heard.

When Brett repeated his question, Meredith realized that she did misunderstand, and she was stunned. "In a moment like this, you want your planner?"

"Meredith, trust me; just do what I ask."

The amazingly dual resurgence and reappearance of the insensitive Brett she so detested left her speechless.

Mumbling her anger, she stormed to the dining room, retrieved the planner from the buffet, and returned in the same manner, shoving it into his stomach, and the breath from him. "Here's your precious planner."

Brett all but folded from laughter, holding his stomach, unable to breathe, his face bluing from lack of oxygen.

"Are we happy?" Meredith punned.

Brett finally recovered his breath. "Perfectly, thank you," he wheezed. "I'm ready for you to open your gift now."

As if inaudibly warned by some unseen force, Meredith and Brett simultaneously focused on the corner of the room next to the palladium windows where Jonah's small body was huddled.

Jonah's face bled anxiety and his voice pleaded: "It's Christmas. Please don't fight."

Crushed, both Meredith and Brett rushed to Jonah. "Oh Jonah, we're so sorry," they apologized, both trying to take the boy into their arms at the same time.

"Don't you love one another?"

Brett's hands gently gripped Jonah's arms. "Hey, Pal. I love this lady more than anything in the whole world."

"Then why are you fighting?"

Brett looked at Meredith. "If she'll just open that little gift box you handed her, she'll find only a small reminder of just how much I really do love and need her."

Now calm, the three sat down in the floor. Brett extended the hand held the box. "I love you, Meredith."

Though excited, Meredith meticulously picked at the tiny box covered with gold paper and tied with red ribbon.

Jonah not only regained his spirit but became impatient. "Open it! Open it!" His excitement bathed Meredith and Brett in the same excitement and Meredith did as Jonah advised, ripping off the paper and opened the box. A green, velvet box carrying its surprise and joy yet remained to be opened.

Meredith slowly pulled open the lid. A rainbow of prismatic light sprayed from a magnificent solitaire diamond…Meredith gasped. Momentarily she didn't understand her emotions because they were both joy and confusion.

Brett removed an like decorated Christmas envelope from the infamous planner and extended it to Meredith. His voice was apologetic. "It wasn't the planner that was important, but the very special envelope inside that I had planned, along with the ring, to give you in front of the entire company's personnel at the Christmas party. I guess for once I did too good a job at hiding what was really at the center of our disagreements. I wanted to do it in front of a world very important to me." Again, tears were unnecessary, because all but chiseled in Brett's face was unmistaken remorse. "A world I found I had made far too important."

Time seemed suspended as Meredith gazed at the envelope silently for a second before gently and lovingly receiving it from Brett's hand. As she read the words, Brett discretely moved to one knee, taking her hand. "As you can see, any kind of explanation for my insistent and even rude conduct would have spoiled the surprise. Even though belated, like the card asks, will you marry me, Meredith?"

Even with all the legal discipline and training she had experienced in holding her emotions at bay, the demands of the whole situation were overwhelming, and she broke down. She dropped the note, covered her face with her hands and bawled like a calf that had lost its mother. No one dared interrupt, for just as the moment had overwhelmed Meredith, it overwhelmed Brett and Jonah as if both coincidentally curved their expressions into a question mark.

Meredith finally calmed. "I...I don't...know."

Brett's expression changed from question to confusion.

Meredith wiped a tear that straggled down her cheek from the previous parade of tears. Surprisingly, she first looked at Jonah, her expression one of consultation, her voice a mixture of chuckle and cry. "Jonah, should I marry this mean old man?"

Jonah picked up the ball glove, again ramming his

hand into its pocket as if to reaffirm his words. "Go for it, Meredith!" Jonah's face became somber. "Mean? He seems like a pretty good guy to me."

It was the first time Jonah had spoken Meredith's name.   She turned to look at Brett.   "If Jonah has determined a preponderance of the evidence exists, I guess I have no choice but accept and agree to marry you, Mr. Brett Collier."

Instantly, Brett rose from the floor, pulled Meredith into his arms, and swirled her in circles, seemingly to the rhythm of Jonah's laughter. The instant her feet retouched the floor, Jonah joined them, all three locked in a single embrace.

"How shall we celebrate this momentous occasion Jonah?"

"What does momentous mean?"

"It means this event has great purpose."

Jonah pointed toward the Christmas Cake perched beneath the glass dome on the crystal pedestal, a treasured piece that had belonged to Meredith's mother. "It looks like it has jewels on top of it," Jonah said.

"It's candied fruit, Jonah."

"Candy! Oh, Boy!"

"Jonah, I've been wanting a piece of this thing since Meredith told me she was making one," Brett added.

Meredith lifted the heavy, glass dome. As she sliced

through the cake, a fresh, fruity aroma filled the room. Meredith precisely plated the slices of cake, and along with a Christmas napkin and fork, served the cake on the dining room table. After a few bites, Jonah took his plate to the accent table left by the large windows the night before. After first eating the candied fruit, he shoved the remainder of his slice of cake into his moth.

"Don't cram your mouth, young man," Meredith admonished.

A rush of sun unexpectedly flooded the room, which drew Jonah's attention through the large Palladium windows and into the park. His face froze in surprise. "Mom!" He turned to Meredith, his face torn in uncertainty. "It's my mom; she's in the park...he hesitated...looking for me!"

The peace and celebration of the moment was suddenly and instantly converted to chaos, and as quickly again ratcheted to bedlam as Jonah rushed the apartment door. Meredith motioned for Brett to stop him.

Jonah struggled in Brett's arms. "Let go or she'll leave me if I don't get down there."

"Jonah, you're going nowhere without your coat. In fact, we're all going," explained Meredith, nervously dialing the phone.

"Jake! Thank God you answered. Don't ask any questions, just get to the park immediately!"

Wisely, Brett donned his own coat before helping

Jonah into his, knowing that the instant Jonah was out of his hands, he would be out the door and gone before Brett could even get into his coat. The two had exited the door as Meredith hurried into her coat, closing the door behind her.

The scene was like the gate opening at the Kentucky Derby, except there were only three contenders, young Jonah the likely winner.   Jonah raced down the short hallway and down the stairs with Brett close behind and Meredith chasing Brett. In their dash across Market Street to the park, Meredith's admonishment to Jonah to 'be careful' went, of course, unheeded.

Meredith's heart palpitated and her unbuttoned coat trailed openly behind her in the cold wind. Jonah leaped into the arms of a chuffy, homeless-looking woman. But it was the woman's male companion that almost sent Meredith's heart into arrhythmia. As Meredith drew closer, her concern with the man's matted mess of hair was quickly replaced by more concern for the German swastikas, vulgar expressions, and symbols of broken crosses displayed on his worn leather coat.

Jonah grasped his Mom's hand, tugging at her. "Come on, Mom. This is your chance to get away from Leo."

"Please, Jake. Where are you?" Meredith prayed, her grip on the button line of her coat as desperate as her prayer that summoned Sgt. Jacob's immediate arrival. "Patience, Meredith. Patience," she whispered. "Don't blow this. They have no idea an officer is coming."Jonah's mother's voice was gritty with anger and four letter curses that would grieve the heart like strong smoke would the lungs. "Jonah, where were you last night? You weren't in the park as I told you to be; and for your information, Leo's a part of this family now."

Jonah's voice was equally angry, ranting, "Mom, he hates me. He curses me. He hits me! He's a jerk! He doesn't love you and he hates me."

Jonah's mother slapped him and his already pink cheeks turned red. "You don't know Leo's feelings."

Jonah glared at his mother as Leo cursed him. He caught the collar of Jonah's coat, which tore, freeing Jonah of his grip. "Come here you little--"

Brett stepped toward Jonah, but Meredith touched his shoulder to wait. "Let him go," Meredith shouted, herself stepping toward Jonah.

Leo smirked and stepped between Meredith, Jonah and his mother. He lustily scanned Meredith head-to-toe. "Where'd you come up with the babe, Jonah?"

Brett stepped in front of Meredith. "Wait just one minute."

Leo's move reflected the sun off an object he was pulling from his pocket. "Brett, he has a knife!" Meredith warned.

The roar of Officer Jacob's squad car pierced the air,

racing through the park's entrance, sliding to a halt. Officer Jacobs' large frame bolted from the cruiser, his baritone voice seemingly matching the roar of his vehicle. "Let the boy go and I'll go easier on you, Leo."

Capitalizing on Leo's momentary distraction, Brett attempted to disarm Leo. With Brett and Leo being about the same size, the momentum and force of Brett's body took both to the ground in a flurry of snow. Jonah's mother attempted to run, but not before she grabbed Jonah's arm, practically dragging him behind her. Meredith mimicked Brett's move, throwing her body at the woman, likewise tumbling the two of them to the ground in a flurry of snow.

The frigid air laced Jonah's scream so that it lingered in the air. "Stop! She may be bad but she's still my, Mom!"

Leo wrestled himself to his feet only to face a bone-crushing blow to the side of his head, and a body slam to the frozen earth by Officer Jacobs. Leo attempted to get up, but Officer Jacobs drove his boot into the cleft of Leo's neck, burying Leo all but face-down in the snow. Leo's cry was pain personified.

Man-handling Leo to his feet, Officer Jacobs also grabbed Jonah's mother by her coat collar. Meredith tried pulling Jonah away from his mother but Jonah fought her, physically and verbally. "Let me go. I hate all of you!"

In response, Officer Jacobs thundered, "You don't want to anger me, son." Jonah's eyes widened, in obvious fear. He calmed as he watched Officer Jacobs handcuff both his mother and Leo. "I didn't know the 'king and queen of felons' were your suspects in question, Meredith."

Brett's struggle to get to his feet was not without reason. For in the spot where he lay, the crimson glow was stark against the white snow. "Brett! You've been stabbed," Meredith cried.

Officer Jacobs was instantly on his two-way radio. "Emergency! I need an ambulance at the south entrance to Central Park. Get another squad car over here as well, ASAP."

Meredith kneeled in the snow, clutching Brett to her, her face inches from his. Like Jonah's words, urgency and frost laced her words. "Brett, hang with me. Hear me? Hang with me!"

Brett's eyes were weakening, became milky, and finally closed.

"No! No! No! This is not going to happen to me again. You can't leave me; you have to live."

Brett's face became static and pale, his body lifeless, Meredith's gloves red with his blood.

Sirens screamed as the trinity of emergency vehicles arrived, an ambulance, a second squad car, and a fire truck. Sirens ground downward, and the air was thick with static and the crackle of radios. Fear and agony played havoc with the very air, but about it ws Meredith's voice, praying as she held Brett's lifeless body in her arms. The wisteria that marked the park with its warmth in summer had become the macabre web of the grim reaper lurking behind its twisted vines.

Seemingly vying for its share of the frosty air was sorrow, its counterpoint melody the unknown tongue-like acronyms voiced by emergency medical technicians communicating with each other and the physician in the emergency room.

Soon, Brett was simultaneously treated and situated securely in the ambulance. Meredith was helped into the ambulance as an officer guided Jonah to the second squad car under the fading voice of officer Jacobs reading Leo and Jonah's mother their Miranda Rights. "You have the right to remain silent. Anything you say may be used against you in a court of law...."

Cold, stunned, numb, and terrorized, Meredith hugged herself tightly as she listened to the emergency medical technicians volley back and forth in a continued, noisy two-way radio exchange with emergency room physicians. Under the roar of sirens, flashing monitors, bleeping medical equipment, IVs swaying from the momentum of the speeding ambulance, and the pungent sting of alcohol, Meredith prayed without ceasing.

The emergency room doors slammed open with a thud against the wall as the medical team pushed into the full energy and chaos normal to the anticipated arrival of an incoming, critical patient. Meredith followed.

A quarterback's handoff could have been no smoother or perfect as a nurse took Meredith's arm and moved her away from the flurry of activity. "You're clothes are a bloody mess, honey; let's get you cleaned up."

"No, I want to stay."

"I know you do, but I also know that you want the patient's needs and the doctor's undivided attention on him right now. I think you understand that. I'm here for you and your needs. Let's get you cleaned up, and then to the kitchen down the hall where there is hot coffee, and...."

"But I don't want any of that. I want to stay right here."

An hour later in the silence of the empty, surgery waiting room steam eddied from Meredith's fourth cup of coffee. She paced, alternating her gaze between the clock on the wall that ticked a melancholy gloom, and the window's view out across the Karns Bridge and the somber Tennessee River that meandered toward the dying, winter sunset.

Meredith was not only torn between her concerns for Brett and Jonah, but failed to fight off the flashback of memory's fingers contending for her mind, a mind that cried years ago in another emergency room when she wanted to watch through the window as physicians worked. Her mind saw herself on the gurney, looking up into the eyes of a physician, his voice rife with hope. "She's with us!" But then her mind went blank again.

Meredith shook the thoughts from her mind, set the coffee on a sofa table and locked herself in her own arms, attempting to calm the persistent shaking she couldn't seem to control.   But then she trembled at the thought of operating tables, scalpels, blood, and the almost panic-like movement of the surgeons and staff.

Doors exiting the surgery department buzzed, grinding their way open. A physician in green scrubs emerged as he untied his surgical mask and removed his scrub hat. Even with scrubs to mute any echo of his steps on the terrazzo floor, they echoed instead a rhythmic, repeated scratchy sound down the long, lonely hospital hallway.

Meredith rose as he approached.

"Ms. McClain, I'm Dr. Sheldon. I understand you're Mr. Collier's fiancée?"

Meredith's reply was weak. "Yes."

"Please sit. My news is positive; Mr. Collier is critical but stable."

Meredith sighed. "Thank God."

"Indeed. Things are looking up, but we must remain guarded; he's by no means out of the woods, yet. We repaired two wounds. One intrusion of the knife's blade barely missed his spleen with significant blood loss, and though the other wound is deep, it is not life threatening. Mr. Collier must have something still unfinished on this earth because he just narrowly escaped death, and by no means am I implying luck. I'm not going to get into technical explanations, but simply state that the fact he's alive is a miracle."

Meredith lowered her face, tears of joy falling into her hands. With a tissue, she touched her nose dry. "Thank you again, Lord."

"I'll have something sent out to calm you."

"No. I'm a little rattled, but I'm okay, doctor."

"With what you've experienced today, your response is only natural." He stood. "He will remain in ICU at least overnight. Then if there are no surprises, and he progresses as we both hope and expect, he will be moved to a room, possibly as early as late tomorrow, more than likely, early evening. I must remind you that you're not going to like what you see, but having gone through what he has, that's expected. Again, I'll be happy to prescribe something for you until you can see your personal physician."

"Thank you, but I'll settle down overnight."

"I'll leave a prescription with the nurse's station just in case. Take it with you when you leave and get it filled in case you do need it. I'll be around again late tonight and in the morning."

Meredith looked into the face of the physician near her own height, but to her he looked like a giant. Her teary eyes looked into the eyes of the man whom God had used to save the life of her husband-to-be. "Thank you so much, Doctor."

"Mr. Collier's a fortunate man, and in more ways than one."

To Meredith, the scene became like a motion picture run backwards; the surgeon's lonely walk down the hall, the double doors reopened, received him and closed again. Her pent-up feelings overflowed and she collapsed onto a chair in tears. Minutes later she had gone to and returned from the restroom more presentable when she heard the voice of Sara Penski.

"M?"

Meredith welcomed Sara Penski into her arms in an embrace that seemed to last forever. Friendship is a wonder and gift from God.

Dark thirty, twenty-four hours later.

Meredith was curled up in the chair in Brett's room, a blanket thrown over her. Brett's groan awakened her and she was at his bedside instantly. That his eyes opened lazily confirmed he remained locked in the grips of sedation.

"Don't try to talk, just relax; I'm here."

His squeeze of her had was languid, he managed a

feeble smile, then again yielded to the power of the medication. Meredith prayed for a moment, returned to her chair, and had covered herself with a blanket when the voice of Officer Jacobs whispered from the door.

"Hey."

Meredith managed a warm smile to the friend who was truly more than friend. "Hello, Jake." She rose from the chair and moved into the officer's waiting arms.

"God bless, Meredith. All our hearts and prayers have gone out for Brett, and you."

"Thank you. He just fell asleep again; let's step into the hallway."

Meredith closed the door behind them. "Thanks for coming, Jake."

"In times like these, being there for one another is the least a true friend can do. I came by last evening, but you were in ICU with Brett. Sara was here and filled me in on the details as best she knew them and I went my way."

"She said you came by. She was here all night, and again today; she left only a few minutes ago."

Officer Jacobs removed his arctic weather cap and coat, and Meredith briefed him on Brett's current condition. "The prognosis is positive but still remains guarded."

"Meredith, you and I know that more than medical science is at work here."

Meredith whimpered. "I couldn't have made it

without faith, Jake."   She crossed her arms and sat in a nearby chair. "Have they found Jonah a temporary home yet?"

Officer Jacobs followed her to a chair. "Yes, in fact both of them."

Meredith's head jerked upward, startled. "Did you say both of them?"

Officer Jacob's dipped his head slightly with a telling smile. "It seems Jonah has a younger sister, Gwen. We found her in the car after you left with the ambulance. Other than being a little scared, she's fine. She's a cute little ten year old, pretty blue eyes, curly blonde--"

Meredith successfully subdued her tendency to commence crying again. "Meredith, I'm sorry. I forgot...I didn't mean...I mean...Richard was my partner. It would be impossible for me to forget him. And Richie wasn't just yours and Richard's son, we all claimed him. We're family."

The huge man pulled Meredith from the chair, gently bringing her face against his barrel chest. The shake of his body told Meredith that he too cried, but silently within.

Meredith pulled back, looked up at Jake and unexpectedly half-laughed. "I hope Gwen's hair and body wasn't as dirty as Jonah's. I had to literally scrub his head to get it clean."

Jake half-laughed as well, and the two were calm in a momentary silence.

"Meredith, I understand your disappointment with the foster child care program, but right now Brett needs you, and all your attention. Jonah and Gwen have both been in temporary homes before so this will be no new experience for them...they'll be fine."

Meredith's eyes widened. "This isn't the first time?"

"I'm afraid not. No offence, but I'm real upset with lawyers and judges. As you know, technicalities govern, and the letter rather than the spirit of the law prevails. Some of these judges seem to hold disdain for the very innocence of the society they represent. Too many are activists, believing they themselves to be the law. Leo should've never been on the street. He's a repeater."

Meredith noted Brett's surgeon coming down the hall and touched Jake's arm. "If you don't mind, grab a cup of coffee while I talk to the doctor."

Meredith observed as the physician meticulously examined Brett. Completing the exam, he silently pondered the sleeping patient a moment before removing his examination gloves and depositing them in the safety disposal.

"The bleeding has stopped. However, I'm going to keep his condition classified as guarded, at least for the moment. These were nasty, all but fatally intrusive wounds." He looked at Meredith. "The kind meant to kill."

Meredith couldn't help but gasp.

"Aside of monitoring him, providing needed medication therapy, and tending his wounds, we've pretty much done what we can do. So, now he needs good nursing and TLC, and then we can release him to you. But first, you need to relax, Ms. McClain, or you won't be able to help him, maybe even find yourself in here as well. I insist that you do the following: accept the prescription I offered, go home, take a long hot shower, and eat a nutritious meal before returning. I know you spent the night in the surgery lounge, which was okay and expected. I'll request a roll away for you tonight; you need the sleep yourself."

Meredith nodded her silent acceptance.

Dr. Sheldon sighed, and chuckled lightly. "In twenty-five years of post residency practice, I've seen it all, Ms. McClain, including—

Meredith interrupted: "Please, call me Meredith."

"Very well, Meredith. I might mention that I have observed you in court. We're professionals, you and I. When others are depending on us, we can't afford to even appear to be overwhelmed. If you must, when you get home, get in your closet and scream as loudly and as long as you like. That helps, at least momentarily."

Meredith managed a chuckle. "You're the doctor."

"Thank you. You would expect the same from me if I were your client."

Sheldon hurriedly wrote another prescription in the

usual illegible scribble, ripped it off the pad and handed it to her. "Add this one to the other. Nothing in here to hurt you, just help you."

As Meredith accepted the prescription, Sheldon gently patted her shoulder and left.

Meredith's prayer was quiet as she ran her fingers through the blonde hair of the man it had been by no means easy to love. She kissed his forehead and whispered, "I love you", then exited the room.

Officer Jacobs hand-crushed the empty Styrofoam cup, dropped it in the trash dispenser next to him, and nudged his large frame away from the wall, anxious to greet Meredith.

"He's still holding his own," Meredith explained.

"What about you, Meredith? How are you doing? I know you're trusting the Lord but are you listening to the Doc?"

"Yes. I accepted a prescription, was told to go home, take a long hot shower and eat a nutritious meal. He ordered a roll away so I will have some facsimile of comfort tonight."

"Good for the Doc. Weather's still bad; I'll give you a lift."

Back in her apartment, the first thing Meredith noticed was the small train spread about on the floor. She didn't return it to the mantle, but to the window sill where Jonah had last played with the train. Still on the accent table was the piece of Jonah's uneaten Christmas Cake, and on the dining room table the remains of hers and Brett's.

Overwhelmed, she plopped down onto the sofa and took one of the several small books of photos from their ornate, oiled walnut case sitting on the coffee table. The photo of Richard and Richie on the sled, smiling, waving, again threw her mind to the past.

"You guys look terrific. Smile," Meredith said, falling over the berm formed by the snow's removal from the driveway early that morning.

Meredith dropped the photo book; the noise returned her mind to the present. She returned the book of photos to the antique box and went to her bedroom. On her knees by the bed, she began: "God, why them? Why us? Why any of it?" She prayed until prostrate, crawled onto the bed, pulled the comforter over her and fell asleep.

The phone rang. Only after several rings did she answer.

"Meredith McClain?"

"Yes."

"Dr. Sheldon here. I'm sorry for interrupting your evening, but I was becoming worried when you had not yet returned to the hospital. We have good news; Brett's condition has improved. Second, are you following my suggested regimen?"

"I had the prescription filled on the way home and wound up falling asleep longer than expected." She crossed her fingers. "I was just getting ready to take that hot shower then have my meal."

"Wonderful. Make sure you do both."

"Thank you for your time, and for being so caring, doctor."

"If I don't see you tonight, I'll see you in the morning, early. Goodnight, Meredith."

The shower water pounded Meredith's head. The streams of hot water washed their way down her body, offering a refreshing massage to her tired frame. The water's gurgle into the shower's drain returned her mind yet again to the day of the accident, and the melting snow running down the gutters with the same gurgling sound as the shower.

"Come on Dad, let's go," Richie shouted, leaving his slice of cake untouched on the table.

"Neither of you even touched your Christmas Cake," Meredith whined.

Richard touched his napkin to his lips, dropped it on the chair, took Meredith in his arms and kissed her long and hard. "I promise the first thing we will do when we come back in will be to devour your always-delicious Christmas cake." He held up two fingers: "Scout's honor."

Richard's passionate kiss was still as fresh in her mind as the day of the accident. Wanting more of the man she so loved, she dropped her arms to her side in disappointment.

"Got your coat on sport?" Richard asked.

"Let's go, Dad."

"This ought to be worth filming, Meredith."

Father and son boarded the small sled, waved, and Meredith commenced capturing the action.

Her body slammed against the cold wall of the shower, mimicked the jolt of her body from her fall over a snow burm and onto the pavement that morning.

Her mind jogged back to the present and Meredith continued the much-needed soaking of both her tired body and stressed mind. She had allowed the hot shower to continue the suggested 15 to 20 minutes Dr. Sheldon had prescribed, then got into her robe. In the kitchen she prepared strong, black coffee, a four oz. salmon steak as her entrée, a side of steamed vegetable, and garlic toast, Richard's favorite. "I miss you all so much," she whimpered.

Meredith lit table candles, turned the TV on, tuned in the seasonal music channel, and took her meal in a quiet that all too soon turned to aloneness.

Fifteen minutes later Meredith forked the last bite of her salmon and steamed vegetables. "Two down and one to go on the doctor's list," she recited aloud, noting the remains of the Christmas cake that she had returned beneath the glass cover on the crystal pedestal. Her heart ached. "It's *déjà vu* all over again. How hard and how many times must such sorrow repeat itself?

She finished her coffee while she gazed through the Palladian windows, revisiting the tragic scene in the park. The dichotomies of life stirred strange emotions within her as she volleyed thoughts of Brett, Jonah, and now his likewise innocent sister, Gwen. "They're just babies," she said. Her lip quivered as she fought back her tears. "That's all I've done for days is cry."

Just as the evening three nights earlier, the seasonal music was interrupted by a National Weather Service announcement: "Arctic-like temperatures will linger through Christmas. Stay inside. If you must drive, do so only in vehicles equipped with chains, or with four-wheel drive. Travel only in an emergency."

"I'm sorry, but this is an emergency," Meredith responded aloud. She donned her favorite winter outfit comprised of two layers of clothing: black corduroy pants, burgundy flannel pants and shirt, two pair of socks and black leather knee-top boots. She stepped into the frigid air. Richard's black, all-wheel drive Toyota Rav 4 sat in frozen silence. Being a police officer, Richard had installed a police scanner in their private vehicle.

The starter dragged, and the vehicle failed to start.

"Come on, this is no time to be obstinate."

The engine fired on what appeared to be its last cranking watt. Meredith sighed relief, turned the radio to Easy Listening, and the spirit of Christmas filled the interior of the vehicle. In sub-freezing temperatures the engine heated slowly. A half-mile passed and the car's heater finally began blowing semi-warm air. Meredith relaxed, driving carefully, but the streets were rapidly becoming heavily covered with new snow. The police scanner's crackle overrode the "Nutcracker Suite" playing on the radio.

The two way radio crackled: "Units in the vicinity of Maire and Forest be on the lookout for two children, a 12-year-old boy and a 10-year-old girl, both reported missing from 1515 Maire, Avenue."

The information outlined in the radio's announcement had been too close a match with Jonah and Gwen to be coincidental, so she hurriedly dialed her mobile phone.

"Jacobs here."

"Jake. Meredith. I'm on the way back to the hospital and heard the scanner...."

"Sorry you heard before I could tell you, Meredith."

She caught her breath. "So it is Jonah and Gwen? Where are you, Jake?"

"North on Hwy. 61, covering an accident. Meredith, they can't get far without us pickin' 'em up. So don't go gettin' yourself upset. Going through your refusal to listen to me once is enough--"

"But Jake, the temperature; it's freezing."

"I'll join the search shortly. Meanwhile, you get yourself to the hospital...and no detours. Understood?"

"But Jake--"

"Meredith! We'll pick 'em up. If I catch you out searching for these kids, I'll haul you in myself. Am I clear?"

Silence.

"Listen to me, Meredith; I gotta go. I'll keep you posted."

"Jake? Jake?"

Exasperated and her emotions torn, Meredith pulled onto the shoulder of the road and began reasoning with herself. "I can't leave Jonah and Gwen roaming around in this sub-zero weather. Where would they go? They have no one." She gripped the steering wheel, resting her forehead against her gloved hands. But her moment of despair became her moment of victory: "Of course, he would come to me." But then she doubted her conclusions when recalling Jonah's having screamed that he hated her. "He didn't mean it. He was just angry."

She sat silent for a moment and accepted the guilt of having evoked such an angry response from Jonah. To that she added the guilt of the warmth and comfort of her surroundings. She had almost succumbed to frustration when a thought thundered into her mind. "He's a smart kid; he would walk the railroad to town. From there he could easily find my apartment."

Meredith turned westward into the blowing snow as she dialed the hospital.

"ICU."

"This is Meredith McClain, code number 4345; may I have the status of Brett Collier, please."

"Stable and resting comfortably, Ms. McClain."

"Thank you. I will not be there for approximately one hour. You have my mobile number if you need me."

Meredith cautiously drove through the mounting snow. Nearing the address of the foster home, the snow was now falling heavily. Though they were faint, she could see blue and red strobes piercing the intensifying snow. As she moved closer, she could see that Officer Jacobs' cruiser was not one of them, so she didn't stop. Instead, she continued cautiously down the street, scanning fence rows, lawns, storage buildings, anywhere two children could hold up possibly unnoticed. Everything was frozen still in the night. "Dear God, they could be hunkered down anywhere," she prayed aloud.

At the bottom of a hill she had managed the sharp, right turn safely, and was alternating her glances between the snowy road in front of her, and the steep embankment to her left. She was both familiar and aware of the absence of a guard rail that defended against the possibility of a 20-foot drop to the railroad below. The falling snow had increased to such intensity that only her familiarity with the road allowed the justification to continue searching the side road. Her mind was so intent she didn't even hear the Christmas Carol, "O Come All Ye Faithful" that played on the radio until the interruption and crack of the police scanner.

"This is Car #2. I'm turning onto Washington Avenue, beginning the search of this area."

The Christmas carol was interrupted, not by the police scanner, but the frightening scratch of the radio broadcast. *"This is the National Weather Service. An added six to eight inches of additional snow accumulation is expected this evening with continued falling temperatures in East Tennessee. A wind chill factor will drop the thermometer to the equivalent of minus twenty degrees. Only emergency travel is advised...."*

Meredith turned her attention to the all but blinding crystalline flakes reflected in the vehicle's headlights, the window fog that was quickly turning to ice, and the resistance of the deepening snow that was opposing the steering of the vehicle. Meredith's conversation with herself seemed to have entreated the very air around her. "Dear God, please let us find them."

A human figure suddenly and unexpectedly darted across the spray of the car's headlights. This caused her to forget that within a very few feet to her left, the railroad was twenty feet below. She reacted naturally and whipped the steering wheel left. Two events resulted: the sickening, thud-like impact of a non-metal object struck the front left of her car, which was followed by the slow tilt of the vehicle, then its sudden, violent somersaulting down the embankment. Meredith's seat was ripped from the car's frame and the driver's door flung open. The seat belt burned its way across her neck as she was jettisoned through the door's opening. Miraculously, she remained belted to the seat. Had she been separated from the seat, the crash of her body onto the rail of the track would have broken her back. In the terrific impact of the seat with the track her mind was again driven to the horrendous impact of the sled that carried her husband and son the day of the fatal accident.

Meredith peered through the lens of the antique, Brownie Hawkeye camera that had belonged to her father.

"The two favorite men in my life look great. All I need is a terrific smile," she begged, to complete the perfect photo.

Meredith had taken one more step backward to widen the camera's angle. The click of the camera's shutter was coincidental with her fall back over the berm of snow created from clearing the driveway earlier in the morning.

"Whoa."

Richard and Richie rushed to Meredith who lay completely still, looking up at them, her blonde hair and embarrassed pink face a stark contrast to the bright snow.

"Have you ever seen the like?" she quipped.

Richard extended his hand. "Not that I recall."

"Mom, you look really funny. You could be in the movies."

"Thanks. I needed that."

"Are you sure you're all right?" Richard asked.

Meredith grasped his hand and he pulled her to her feet, again kissing her hard and deep. "You wear embarrassment well; it's actually becoming on you."

"Maybe I should fall more often."

Meredith's reach to put her arms around her husband's neck was unfulfilled as he turned to Richie. "Last one to the sled's a rotten egg."

The two ran at breakneck speed for the shiny, oak sled parked next to the steep driveway that led to the rural road.

"Dad's the rotten egg," Richie shouted, his arms raised in victory.

"Okay. No rubbing it in," Richard said, straddling the sled behind Richie. Richie snuggled his back to his father's chest.

"One more shot," Meredith called.

The two riders smiled and waved as Meredith clicked

the camera a second time. "Got it!"

Meredith slapped the snow from her earmuffs and slid the camera into the pocket of her blue, quilted winter sport jacket as Richard's baritone voice boomed, "Here we go." Richie followed with, "We're off."

Richard pushed the sled off with his heels, and the two began the drop down the steep drive and their voices lingered in the cold air like the blue smoke of fall.

"Please be careful," Meredith shouted, clapping her hands.

"Always," Richard's voice responded as the sled moved down the rural road, increasing both its distance and speed. Meredith followed to the road, waving.

Her joy turned to sheer terror when a battered, green truck spun out of control from a side road onto the main road at the bottom of the hill.

"Richard!   Richard!" Meredith screamed, running down the hill while attempting to keep from falling on the slick road. But her feet slipped from beneath her, and for a second she appeared to levitate above the pavement's thin sheet of ice and snow. Her head and body slammed to the pavement, leaving her unable to see the battered truck's continuing wild and out of control weave, and the sled's rapid decent on its collision course with the vehicle.

The police report revealed the inebriated driver's mind to be so numb his control of the vehicle was impossible, possibly even incapable of discerning the small, oncoming sled.

A blast of snow in Meredith's face brought her mind back to the present. The pain in her memory, and in her body were too much, and everything went black.

Meredith awoke, still belted to her seat, in the same position on the railroad. She had no idea how long she was unconscious, only that her body was covered with a thin layer of snow. The burn on her neck was still hot and excruciating, as was the pain radiating from her left leg, which she discovered she could not move. The ice-cold metal object beneath and along side her body and head she assumed to be one rail of the dual-spine of the tack's steel rails. Extreme pain was now centered in her lower right leg.

Panic overtook Meredith. "My God, I'm literally on the railroad with my leg broken. Help! Help!" she screamed.

The only sound in the bitter cold besides her unheeded voice was the wind whistling through the crumpled vehicle a few feet away, and the occasional crackle of the police scanner that apparently still worked.

She had raised herself, only to be greeted by a spike in the already excruciating pain. A small body was frozen in the reflecting spray of the vehicle's still functioning headlights. The form moved ever so slightly. Meredith pushed her personal pain to the back of her mind.

"God help me; I've hit someone," she cried. "I must

get to my phone."

Her first attempt to drag herself to the car resulted in pain so fantastic she almost passed out.

"Give me strength, Lord. I have to do this."

Disregarding the horrific pain, she repeated her attempt to drag herself toward the vehicle. Time seemed interminable, the effort required almost beyond human. But in the passing minutes, and after more agonizing pain from her movement, she peered through the vehicle's glassless window. Her mobile phone was holstered in its metal case, the green power light bright. "It's still functional."

She had maneuvered her arm through the window, crying both from pain and exasperation: "I can't reach it."

An umbrella lay near the door. "I don't know," she cried, and broke off the end of a small, dead tree branch picking at her hair. She placed it between her teeth and bit down hard to counter the anticipated pain from another attempted reach for the umbrella. She got the umbrella, but each swipe of the umbrella at the phone brought agonizing pain so great that her bite severed the small stick held between her teeth. She collapsed back in the snow, her frustration competing with the pain.

"Lord, I need you!" she voiced, beginning to cry, and the more she cried the more gripping her anger and frustration became. "Come on, God, can't you see I need a little help here?"

She remembered Sara's chuckling comment about existential Christianity, but any laughter was impossible. "Was Sara right? Where is my faith?" Her monologue seemed only to intensify the silence when a strange sound interrupted. It was a child's whimper.

She listened closely, but the broken transmission of the police scanner interrupted. She attempted to listen again. Only silence.

"Hello!" Her voice and breath died quickly in the almost glacial-like air. A stir at the front of the vehicle revealed the teary, blue-eyed face of a curly blonde-haired girl peeping around the crumpled metal.

"Are you all right?" Meredith asked.

The girl stared in silence and only whimpered.

"I'll bet your name is Gwen?"

The child nodded a slow affirmation.

"Oh dear, God. Gwen, that's Jonah on the bank isn't it?"

The girl again nodded the affirmative, but she spoke. "He can't move his arm, and he can't stand; he's dizzy."

New hope exploded adrenalin into Meredith's veins. "Gwen, you have to help so we can all get to safety before we freeze. Understand?"

Gwen nodded.

"My leg is broken. Will you be my arms?"

"Yes."

"Come here."

Cautiously, Gwen crawled to Meredith.

"The top of the car is crushed too much for me to pull myself through the window."

Meredith pointed inside the car. "The green light is a mobile phone. Try to crawl through the window on the passenger's side and get the phone."

"Okay," the little ragamuffin said through chattering teeth before she disappeared around the front of the vehicle. Meredith's mind returned to her own pain, and she noticed that her voice atomized in the dense polar-like air. Gwen's face peered through the window on the passenger's side. The window frame was not crushed, but jagged glass remained around its edges.

"You'll have to break the rest of the glass out of the window, Gwen. Find a stone."

Gwen disappeared for a moment then reappeared holding a round, river stone. "Is this big enough?"

"Yes. Pull your hands into your coat sleeves and hold the stone with your coat as you strike the window."

Gwen's punch was insufficient to break the glass.

"Harder, Gwen!" Meredith encouraged.

The next strike had cleared the window of the glass.

"Good girl."

Gwen had crawled only partially through the window when she complained: "My leg is caught."

"Does it hurt?"

"No."

"Great. When I push the umbrella toward you, grip it and pull but only if it doesn't hurt." Meredith and Gwen pulled themselves forward simultaneously. The tearing sounds of Gwen's clothes pierced the still quiet as Meredith cried, "My leg." She collapsed back into the snow. As crushed by her disappointment as her leg, she again verbalized her anger. "What's it going to be next, God?"

She gritted her teeth to prepare for the pain she knew would assault her again as she attempted to raise her body. "Meredith's so sorry, Gwen. I shouldn't have said that."

Gwen extended her body and arm as she reached for the phone. "I can reach it now."

The shift of Gwen's weight, however, apparently upset the delicate balance of the vehicle, and it began to move.

Meredith screamed. "Gwen, don't move! If the car rolls, we both will be crushed."

Meredith's scream startled Gwen, and she dropped the phone, which Meredith watched fall to the gear shift's boot. Her pain was so severe, she momentarily lost focus.

Gwen fell forward and her weight shifted the car's delicate balance, but the vehicle inched slightly over but failed to roll.

Meredith's agonizing cry was now a wail, and in the

sub-zero air, the breath of her lament was seemingly encrusted in the white condensation that lingered in the air from her breath.

Suddenly the car's lights extinguished, plunging the scene into darkness.

"Oh no, what else?"

Meredith broke off another piece of the limb and tucked it between her teeth to grit against the pain, then continued her attempt to crawl into the window as far as possible, but her clothes caught and stopped her movement. Her thoughts were obliterated by a new and horrible sound, that of a moving mechanical noise.

Red and blue strobes suddenly painted the trees as a vehicle stopped on the road above. Doors slammed and Meredith heard voices.

"Down here, on the railroad," she shouted.

Never had there been a time when shuffling snow, heavy grunting, and lungs pulling oxygen had sounded so wonderful. Several voices mumbled as they descended the steep, twenty-foot embankment.

"Stabilize the vehicle," one voice ordered. Two others groaned, grappling with the underbrush to get to the vehicle.

More flashing strobes appeared from an emergency vehicle and another police cruiser. Spotlights fanned the surrounding area like shadows from the blades of a helicopter. The voice of Officer Jacobs was familiar: "Meredith, are you all right?"

"Jake, Jonah's in front of the car on the bank."

"Spread out. There's a boy somewhere in front of the car," Jakes voice shouted.

"We see him," came a reply.

Meredith watched Jake labor around the vehicle to evaluate the situation. He dropped to his knees beside her.

Meredith's voice was weak. "Where have you been? I was beginning to give up hope." She wanted to cry, but instead she garnered the strength to try to appear not frightened.

Jacobs pushed his face close. "I don't know whether to celebrate with a kiss, or slap you for failing to heed my warning. You're a crazy woman, Meredith McClain."

"The boy's all right; it's only a broken arm!" a paramedic shouted.

"Gwen's on the other side of the car, Jake."

"We got her," a voice shouted.

Jacobs turned his face away, looking into the heavens as if to conceal his own frustration then turned back to Meredith. "Yea, and if you'd listened to me, these kids might not have been alive."

"Jake, I hit Jonah. Suddenly he was in front of me, and..."

"Yes, but had you not found them, they would have

died out here, both of 'em, so knock off the guilt stuff; that's an order."

For a second, Meredith was able to feel something above the pain. But the menu of sounds, the short and loud blast of a horn, the clang of a bell, and a growl that shook the ground left no question that it was a train that approached. It had turned Meredith's pain from physiological to psychological.

"We gotta get 'em out of here, and now!" Jake shouted.

Motion and panic shifted the weight of the car.

"Look out! The car's going to tumble," an EMT shouted.

Jake tried wedging his huge frame against the vehicle to allow the others to extract Meredith.

Even as the EMT team extracted her from the vehicle, the car shifted and rolled, coming to rest on its top on the track.

Jake and two EMTs lifted Meredith to safety on the bank as the train's searching spotlight highlighted the track, bearing down no more than half the length of a football field away. The multiple engine growled its brakes, the roar all but deafening. Still, the roll and mechanization of tons of steel bulldozed into the car, a shrill, grinding noise as the train pushed the vehicle down the tracks.

3:00 p.m. December 21ˢᵗ
Park West Hospital
Knoxville, Tennessee

Oxygen bubbled from a wall unit and the beep of machines monitored vital statistics defining anything that described other than what would be identified as 'ambiance'. It was the sound of a watch, a guard, a sentry defending the camp from the enemy. A human guard is also present, towering above Meredith's hospital bed—an out-of-uniform Officer Jacobs.

Sara Penski occupied the oversized lounge chair in a corner of the room, her charcoal sweater pulled to the elbows that rested on the knees of her wool, gray pants. Her face was buried in the palms of her hands.

"Sara?"

Sara instantly joined Jake at bedside and worked her fingers through his. Jake touched his other hand to Meredith's, bowing his head. His lips quietly moved as he prayed silently.

Sara's eyes were so tightly clinched they seemed to form crevices in her almost flawless complexion.

"And amen," Jake concluded audibly.

Sara leaned her head against Jake's shoulder. "I don't understand. Why are seemingly a certain few handed so much?"

"Well, because our understanding is neither required nor necessary, only our 'faith', and that in the fact that 'God's will is done'. Our responsibility is the exhibition of a faith unchanged by circumstance."

Brett hobbled into the room. Harrison Copeland, CEO of <u>Fiber Optics</u>, and wife, Maggie, waved modestly and reverentially from the other side of the glass wall.

Brett touched Meredith's face, attempting to squelch his tears. Jake rested his large palm on Brett's shoulder. "If anyone can pull through this, Meredith can. I've never known anyone stronger, nor with more determination. God's purpose drives this lady, and I believe her work has only begun."

Brett's reply was broken. "Why do we not realize what we have until we're threatened with its loss?"

"If anyone understands that, Meredith does," Sara interjected.

"This thing isn't over." Even in a whisper, the voice of the gentle giant seemed to resonate. "Who knows what will be the end result?" Sensitive to Brett's countenance remaining downtrodden, Sara pushed an arm around Brett in support. "You're not really sufficiently recovered yourself," she consoled, assisting him to the oversized lounge chair.

"I know, Sara. But the pain in my body in no way compares to the agony in my heart. I've been such a fool, so self-centered. I just pray she will forgive me."

Sara kneeled by Brett, pulled his hand from his forehead and took it in hers. "Now listen to me, Brett Collier. I've know Meredith McClain a long time, and I know that you are the most important person in her life; she loves you very much."

She lifted Brett's chin, forcing him to look at her. "I'm not going to lie to you and tell you she didn't have concerns about you. I did, and I expressed them rather forcibly. But you know what? She countered me, and with reasons real, true, and good. She reminded me of times critical to her when you stood by her. Not only that, the Brett you have become proves the same Brett lives inside, something she believed all along. The caring, loving Brett she believed in was indeed there all the time, as she believed he was. You two are going to do just fine. The future is yours and what you make of it."

12:00 noon
New Years Eve
Claremont Children's Home

If there was ever anything more beautiful than the spacious, two-story log cabin tucked snugly among

Tennessee hardwoods, it was the icicles hanging from the fascia boards, and the green wreaths that seemed to want to narrow the distance between them and snuggle to each other on the second story dormers. The winter picture was complete, down to the blue smoke, having left its warmth within the cabin, curled out of the stone chimney, kissing the white pines on its journey upward.

Inside, the cabin was filled with children's voices singing the carols of Christmas. The fragrance and sound that popped and crackled from the hickory logs roaring in the huge stone fireplace filled the large dining room. Across the hand-hewn, cherry mantel, a white banner scissored from red construction paper read: *He came upon a midnight clear*. Thick, pine greenery ran the length of the 10-foot mantel, sprinkled with red Nandina berries picked in the prime of their maturation and color, and iridescent lights danced on the garland like some exotic ballet company.

A seven-foot, white pine Christmas tree stood in and out of the way in an adjacent corner. The signature of the young hands that decorated it gave the tree its beauty: six pointed stars, aluminum foil tinsel, quilted dolls, velvet-like bows and ribbons made from scrap cloth, and tens of feet of stringed popcorn. Decorative balls made of real mistletoe dangled from door-frames.

Fifty children filled the home's large dining room built to accommodate closer to 35. Meredith, Brett, and officer

Jacobs looked on with fellow officers, EMT, and fireman who participated in the now famous rescue broadcast by the nation's newspapers, television and cable networks across the nation.

Meredith wore a Christmas-red blouse and a heritage green, wool skirt that concealed her leg cast. Brett's bandages were also concealed beneath a designer, pine green shirt, the knot of his tie a half Windsor, to which Meredith objected. Only the brevity of time to prepare had allowed it to pass unchanged. Assured was that zero reminders of the still-present and unhealed physical debilities were visible.

Claremont's mayor, city council members, and local media were present, and of course, Ira and Miriam Ingram, founders and caretakers of Claremont Children's Home.

Strangely, Sara Penski, who had hardly left Meredith's side since the terrifying night, was absent.

Ira Ingram quieted the crowd that talked in a low rumble of conversation. "Let us continue our program with the reading of the Christmas Story by one of our very special guests, Meredith McClain."

Meredith opened Brett's Christmas present, the wide margin bible she had coveted for so long. "I will be reading from Luke, Chapter two, verses one through fourteen."

"And it came to pass in those days that there went out a decree from Caesar Augustus that all the world should

be taxed...."

Every eye was fixed on Meredith, even the small children whose attention was not always available. Each and every person listened as the important passages were succinctly and dramatically read that described the first Christmas. At the concluding 'Amen', the roar of conversation returned as if turned up by a rheostat.

Ira Ingram slapped his hands together loudly. "Okay, all children in front of the fireplace for a group photo." The call ratcheted the volume of the children's excitement to exuberance.

"Children, quietly, please." Miriam Ingram's voice was soft, but the children responded accordingly.

"We would like to ask Meredith, Brett, our police, EMT, and firemen guests to all join us in the group photo, please."

Hesitant, Brett and Meredith finally hobbled to join the group, but only after Ira's insistence.

Strobes flashed and dazzled the children's eyes, again arousing their excitement. After the photographer had successfully captured both moment and meaning, she declared, "I believe we have it."

Officer Jacobs crossed the room and opened the front door. "Well, look who we have here."

Sara Penski entered, wearing a Christmas red top coat, a green wreath on its lapel. The Ingrams greeted her as well and returned to their position at the fireplace. "We're so glad each one of you could find your way free to attend today. We know it took both sacrifice and cooperation, and even more importantly, we know within our hearts it is an indication of the love for Claremont Children's Home. We are so thankful to celebrate our twenty-fifth Christmas."

His momentary pause obviously reflected that much more could be said but that the following would have to suffice.

"Times have changed and funding is becoming more difficult, complicated by both time and circumstance. Still, the successful efforts in facilitating the life-saving extension on our mortgage mandated that, out of respect, we postpone our annual Christmas party so that all those responsible could join us in our celebration, and for us to publicly show our gratitude. With that said, the only thing remaining is for all this beautiful food on these tables to be received with thanksgiving and supplication."

Sara stepped forward. "Excuse me for interrupting, Mr. Ingram, but we have a Christmas card that has a very special message for you, Mrs. Ingram, and the Claremont Children's Home."

Meredith looked toward Sara and raised a questioning brow. Sara walked to the fireplace where the Ingrams turned the floor over to her. From beneath her coat Sara retrieved a thick, standard #10 envelope.

Meredith crossed her arms and curled her face into quandary.

Ira Ingram received the envelope, his hand searching his red and black checked flannel shirt.   He turned to Miriam: "Mother, I seemed to have misplaced my glasses. Would you read...."

"I'm sorry, but I don't have my glasses either."

"I guess that leaves you, Miss Penski. Please read for us, dear." Ira Ingram pushed his arm around his wife to await the reading of the contents of the envelope. Rather than a Christmas card, Sara pulled what appeared to be a half-inch thick document.

"My, my, I have never seen a Christmas Card that required so much writing," Miriam Ingram declared, laughing.

To: Claremont Children's Home & Mr. & Mrs. Ira Ingram:

The unselfish and charitable attitude and contribution of Claremont Children's Home to the children, and the town of Claremont cannot be allowed to go unnoted, or unheralded, and especially, unrewarded.

Fiber Optics Corporation and its employees are pleased to announce that the attached legal document guarantees not only the current financial solvency of Claremont Children's Home, but for years to come.

Please accept our apologies for being unable to attend, and receive Brett Collier as our representative, whom we wish to thank for bringing to our knowledge the needs that not only exist with this home, but that have existed for too long.

> Merry Christmas, and God bless,
> Harrison Copeland,
> CEO Fiber Optics, Inc.
> and Mrs. Margaret Copeland

As the Ingrams tended their tear-stained faces, Sara Penski revealed yet another envelope as she gazed at Meredith, who inhaled and extended an expression of question. "I seemed to have forgotten there is another letter, this one for Meredith."

Meredith lifted her hands to express her confusion as she hesitantly stepped forward, received and opened the envelope. "I don't know about this, but I will deal with you later, Penski," she said, opening the envelope. When she looked at the letter, she cleared an already full throat.

The moment was interrupted, however, by yet another knock on the front door. Officer Jacobs moved to answer, all while not taking his eyes off Meredith. "For some reason, I feel that we need to answer the door before we continue," he said, an undeniable smirk on his face.

Jonah and Gwen entered, and Officer Jacobs removed their coats. Jonah wore a Chestnut suit, white shirt and tie, Gwen a white dress with a red bow at the throat, her blonde curls tied back in a white ribbon. She could be described only as, adorable.

Meredith attempted to control her tears, motioning the two to come to her, but Officer Jacobs placed his huge hands on their shoulders, staying their momentary advancement. "We're fine right where are for now. Sorry for the interruption; you may continue, Meredith."

Meredith was unable to read. Brett came to her side, pushed his arm around her and kissed her on the cheek. "You can do this." Meredith began:

> To: Meredith:
>
> Knowing of your recent sacrifice and noble deeds, when Harrison and Maggie showed us the beautiful Crystal Lighthouse hostess gift given them for the party you were never able to attend, I had to acknowledge the Divine love that obviously powers the life you live that is indeed a lighthouse, one I hope in the future shines forth from us all.
>
> Brett had asked that I commence the adoption process for Jonah and Gwen, depending upon your approval, of course. All the papers lack is your signature. You will make a wonderful family. Thank you for who you are and what you do,
>
> R. Samuel Denver, Esquire
>
> P.S. Please note the papers designate that the parties to this agreement are Mr. Brett and Mrs. Meredith Collier. If this document is acted upon with this inaccurate designation, I will be guilty of fraud.

Meredith turned to Brett only to find herself engulfed in his arms. Officer Jacobs released Jonah and Gwen to run to the couple who instantly broke their embrace to take the two children into their arms.

Officer Jacobs lifted his cup of hot cider. "May I

have your attention, please. Before we indulge in the bounty awaiting us on these tables wherewith we have been so blessed, I would like to make a toast: "To Him who wondrously watches over us in all things." He took a swallow of the cider, then immediately launched his deep, baritone voice into a stanza of, "O Come All Ye Faithful"; everyone joined the singing.

After sharing the bounty of the Christmas meal, Brett and Meredith stood in front of the three Christmas Cakes she had prepared; Sara joined them to slice the third cake.

"Jonah, no cramming," Meredith reprimanded politely, pointing to her mouth.

"I wasn't going to miss getting to eat my cake this time," he said.

It seemed everyone laughed as Jonah finally swallowed the mouthful of cake.

"Yuck!" Gwen said, pulling a partially massacred piece of a gold-foiled coin from her mouth; she placed it in Meredith's cupped hand. "What is it?" she asked.

"Look everyone. Gwen's slice of cake had one of the two good luck coins that were secretly placed in each of the cakes. Those having the coins in their slice of cake will have good fortune in the coming year," Meredith explained.

The small girl's ponytail bounced, and her blue eyes sparkled as she moved between Meredith and Brett, each edging an arm around her. Jonah removed an ornament from the Christmas tree, returned to the table and shoved yet another huge bite into his mouth and again drew Meredith's reprimand.

"Jonah, if the coin was in your cake you could have swallowed it without even knowing it."

Jonah took Meredith's other hand and looked up at her. "Yes I would."

"And how do you figure that?"

He handed her the small ornament of the Little Drummer Boy. "Because I'm the Little Drummer Boy, and it's a miracle Christmas."

Epilogue

The true miracles of life extend beyond the visible healing of a broken and maimed physiology, and therefore almost always invisible and not discernable to a far too busy world. That doesn't make them nonetheless real, but the spiritual witness of 'charity', the divine benevolence of God that arms or super weapons, individuals or armies, kings or kingdoms can destroy. It is a unique, divine body, not among man, but within the souls of believing man, an eternal flame invisible and invincible, created and sustained only by the breath of God.

Ω